The Sanctuary Knocker

by **Sam J. Stewart**

The Sanctuary Knocker

Text Copyright © 2018 Sam J. Stewart
Cover © 2018 Sam J. Stewart

The moral right of the author has been asserted

All rights reserved. No part of this publication may be reproduced, stored in a retrieval system, or transmitted in any form or by any means, electronic, mechanical, photocopy, recording or otherwise, without prior written permission of the copyright owner. Nor can it be circulated in any form of binding or cover other than that in which it is published and without similar condition including this condition being imposed on a subsequent purchaser.

All correspondence regarding this novel should be addressed to:
samstewart9669@gmail.com

tel: +44 (0)7858 575927

Sam J. Stewart was raised in Co. Tyrone, Northern Ireland.

His father was a local entrepreneur and holder of ancient market rights near the town of Dungannon. These rights allowed him to charge a toll of every commercial vehicle coming to the cattle market in his village. As a young man, he was an adept in the sport of road-bowling. After a life in the public eye, he died in poverty.

Sam's mother was a primary school teacher. An inoffensive woman, she died of cancer when Sam was eleven.

He boarded at St. Patrick's College, Armagh where hunger and the regime fostered in him a response of borderline kleptomania. At 19 he attended Belfast College of Business Studies where he learned about women and self-sufficiency. He played Gaelic football and piano and was averagely good at both.

Over the following thirty years he drifted from job to job without leaving any particular mark on society. At the age of fifty, he discovered his *milieu* in the company of horses. He now runs a thoroughbred stud farm in the south of England.

He is a playwright and novelist.

The Sanctuary Knocker

The Complete
O'Toole

A series of three novels following the fortunes of Dublin detective Turlough (Toby) O'Toole

'The Druid'
'riverRunner'
'The Sanctuary Knocker'

O'Toole, a man ill-equipped to deal with events beyond the normal, encounters an extraordinary figure in *The Druid* and is led into a world of international politics, land agitation and murder.

———-------

Available on Kindle and in paperback on Amazon.

———-------

By the same author:

Plays -
The Party (2018)
Les Grotesques (2020)

The Sanctuary Knocker

'The ruins of time build mansions in eternity'
　　(W.B. Yeats – Foreword, Cú Chullain of Muirthemne)

INTRODUCTION

Following his expulsion from the Irish police force for the sin of hubris, the headstrong but hapless O'Toole flees to the remoteness of Belize in an effort to outrun his demons. He's not hard to find; Interpol have a warrant out for him and he is tracked down by the British Security Service (MI5) who render him to London, believing he has the inside track on The Druid, the fanatical priest and mastermind behind 'unrelenting psychological warfare against Britain'.

The Druid and his acolytes hijack a scientific research vessel at the mouth of the Thames and sail upriver towards the City of London, anchoring opposite the Houses of Parliament. They threaten the British with the release of a deadly bacterium unless the Prime Minister assents to a clandestine meeting, knowing that the existance of the amoeba permanently shifts the balance of relationships between Ireland and Britain. British irregulars attack the ship and a gunfight ensues, with drastic consequences.

Resisting interrogation, and with The Druid now incarcerated in Broadmoor High Security Psychiatric Hospital, O'Toole forswears his former life and returns to Ireland with the help of his friend Doreen Downey ('D.D.') who finds him a flat and a job in the seaside town of Bundoran in Donegal. He now looks forward to a quiet life...

The Sanctuary Knocker

Chapter 1

O'Toole had driven sixty miles to open the envelope. Making sure the waitress wasn't looking, he drew the envelope from an inside pocket. He already knew what was in it. *'To be opened only in the event of my death'*. He quickly turned the envelope over and placed it face down on the table. He was getting nervous. He ordered another coffee. Black, one sugar.

His mother was born and raised here, in a bad stone cottage somewhere in these scrubby hills. She encountered a man. His people went on to become big builders in England. From his bag he took a ginger nut biscuit. He always had biscuits with his coffee.

He could give the envelope to the police; that would be the correct thing to do. He'd be off the hook. The deaths caused would not be on his head. He walked round the village for fifteen minutes, then he drove back to Bundoran and hid the envelope. In case they'd be looking for it.

The following evening, a nine o'clock quiet descended upon Cookstown, a stout commercial centre in County Tyrone. The remaining cars seeking to escape the curfew were making their way out. A slow, ageing man in a hi-vis jacket waited to bring the barrier down at the Dungannon Road, saluting the drivers as they passed. He secured the barrier with a light combination lock and shuffled off to the pub to watch the darts competition.

Around fifteen minutes later, the sound of a heavy diesel engine offended the late summer stillness. There was a cracking and a crashing followed by shouting and revving car engines.

In the pub, someone shouted "It's a digger!" Three men ran out of the pub to see the barrier splintered and a digger roaring down the main street followed by four cars. The cars were sporting flags out the windows and two more flags flew atop the digger. The three men ran after the convoy, then thought the better of it and turned to run to their own cars. The barrier-man got on his phone to summon help.

The digger then turned on the wide main street and came straight for the pursuing vehicles while the rest of the convoy sped down the town. The lead car was caught by the bucket of the digger and ground to a halt. Two men jumped out of the digger with cudgels and started beating on the windscreen of the damaged car. The other two pursuers stopped at a safe distance to shout invective at the cudgel men. They got back into their digger and headed off towards the roundabout and the Tullywiggan Road.

The convoy turned into Burn Road and stopped at the town hall. A bundle of men got out and untied the rope on the flag pole, lowered the Union Jack flag and detached it, then fixed their own flag and hoisted it to the top of the flag pole where it flopped, listless. They took photographs and laughed for their cellphone recordings, then fled in convoy down the Coagh Road as defenders arrived at the broken barrier.

He lived above the shop in a square, boxy flat. Not very inspiring, but comfortable enough. And if he got bored, he could go out and walk the strand, away from the noise of the tourist shops and the penny arcades.

Recently he had been pondering the possibility of getting a dog. Small enough, but not clingy or yappy; maybe a Spaniel. The obvious considerations; who would look after the dog when he was away? Could he keep it with him in the shop? The customers might take to him. A dog would reflect his personality. A few years ago he might have been fairly certain of his attributes; now he might need a second opinion. The dog would warn off intruders.

Amid such musings, he also thought of how he had arrived at his current situation and where he would be if he went along with DD's plans for his political future. He was getting old. Soon there would no longer be the opportunity, or the time, to try things for fun. He would have to fix the remaining course of his life, think about retirement and a pension.

At the strand he skimmed a few stones and thought about the time he holidayed in Sicily, found a beach all to himself, and then forgot to go swimming. Silly. That would be one of his remaining goals; to rectify that, to go swimming in Sicily. Whether alone or in company didn't matter.

Next morning at work, he was mildly surprised to be greeted by the Second Violin of the National Symphony Orchestra, as she had been in just last week and had bought an illustrated book on L.S. Lowry and his intriguing 'matchstick men'. She came to say good morning and introduced herself as Maire ni Raighbheartaigh. They discussed the Lowry (with which she was very pleased) and he agreed the work was very attractive and evoked suitably Blake's *'dark Satanic mills'*.

She was going off horse-riding on the beach at Rossnowlagh with some friends. Did he like horse-riding? O'Toole, with a slightly embarrassed smile, agreed he used to ride but following a fall in Wicklow a couple of years ago had suffered a loss of nerve. "That's a pity," she said, "but maybe you could join us some time in the future?" He thanked her for her consideration and as she was about to leave she added "Our string quartet is giving a recital in Sligo on Saturday evening. Would you come?"

O'Toole hadn't been on a social engagement since his visit to DD's house for a weekend in Derry two years ago. He was still feeling fragile and not at all confident, so he hesitated. "No pressure," she said, as if she knew. "Just a glass of wine and some Schumann. I think you'd enjoy it."

She placed two tickets on the counter top. "Come alone or bring a friend. It would be nice to see you there." She gave him a gracious smile and departed.

O'Toole was grateful she was gone as it allowed him to collect himself. He hadn't expected this, and found himself irritated and at a disadvantage, but as the day wore on he got back on an even keel and even began to consider her motives. She was, it must be said, a pleasant woman, and very handsome. She was evidently talented and probably good company. He would decide later.

At noon, Daithi put a call through to him; it was DD. Could they meet for coffee at 4 p.m? She was down for the day from Derry. "Surely. Come to the bookshop. Daithi can take over for an hour."

O'Toole had to give some thought to her visit. He was in a position where he was beholden to her for a lot after his life and career as a policeman had gone to pieces, and was further compounded by the shattering loss of a woman with whom he was deeply in love. DD had helped him to pull himself together and got him the job in the bookshop, and the flat.

And yet she was instrumental in his fall from grace. Once, just a good friend going back years, she had suckered him into involvement in one of the most notorious political and criminal cases in recent history. And being the trusting patsy he was, his ruin was total in the aftermath. Now he was a fragile husk, trying to avoid involvement as a man with sciatica avoids sudden movement.

She had changed. She used to be fun, with a good citizen's interest in the future of the country – they had met at a political rally in Dublin all those years ago – but now she was so intensely political he couldn't tell if she was still a friend or still using him.

In fact, maybe she hadn't changed at all. Maybe the Good Citizen had always been a calculating extremist with more than a passing familiarity with mayhem and murder.

She would want something, that was for sure. He didn't want to think about politics. He was weary. He had witnessed the bombing of the research ship Cupp with the Irish fellows on board outside parliament in London. He had seen the murder of O'Neill and the attempt on the life of Father Doherty on the London Eye – *after a guarantee of safe passage*. He remembered his disgust for the base British at that time, but he was too strung out to do anything about it. And they would be watching…

She greeted him warmly, with a kiss on the cheek. She was still a very pretty woman, even though, like himself, she was showing her age. Character lines at the sides of her eyes. He could still remember how she took the light out of his eye at their first committee meeting to organise a commemoration of the anniversary of the 1916 Rising. No make-up, no airs, just a lovely, gay, yellow-haired force of nature. And happily married.

The grown children were all well, she agreed. Husband Jim - 'The Thatch' (don't ask) - had taken to wine-making and the house was full of beakers and barrels and bubbles. The children had pronounced on his efforts.'Yeukkk!'

There would be busy times ahead. We were going to stir the pot. He would be surprised at the level of planning. The Brits were in bits. The Unionists were on their last legs. Nationalists were winning the vote, and the P.R. The big push was on.

"We want you to speak at a rally."

"What! Why?"

"Because of who you are."

"Who am I? A de-frocked policeman!"

"You're more than that. You know The Druid. You're famous. And you have the letter."

"I'm an Untouchable! I have no credibility anywhere. And you can have the blasted letter if you want."

"No I don't. He gave it to you. And that gives you an *awful* lot of credibility."

O'Toole was incensed. He wanted a quiet life. "Look, I told you at the time it would take time to recover. I understand that," she said, "but remember what you felt like when they blew up the Cupp. You knew it was time to make a choice. We have them on the run. Just make the speech. There'll be others to help you. We'll tell you what to say. We'll give you the speech in advance."

"I'm no good at public speaking. I've only ever talked down to junior cops."

"Let me give you a tip; talk down to your audience. Despise them! Then you'll have no problem talking at them. Pretend they're cops." She smiled.

It is unlikely that the spirit of hubris which had contributed to his downfall would ever trouble him again, so it was only apprehension that governed his thoughts when presented with an opportunity to come out of his self-imposed exile and make a statement of his political beliefs that he thought had died in his twenties.

With the order from Doreen Downey to speak at The Movement parade in Galway and the invitation from Maire ni Raighbheartaigh to the string quartet, O'Toole's social life would require a significant adjustment. In his current frame of mind, he was doubtful he could successfully negotiate either engagement. If he choked at Galway, it would be a severe embarrassment; if he went to the musical evening, he would inevitably have to converse with the musicians – four women – and appear normal.

But he was not normal. He was a man who had barely escaped jail for conspiracy in Italy and who was implicated by association in an attempt on the life of the king of England! Good God, he was a country policeman, or had been. An ordinary fellow who worked in a bookshop. And unlucky in love to boot, but that wasn't unique.

And what were the locals in Bundoran saying about him? Everyone knew. He was famous. It had been all over the media for months. Yet they said nothing, which only proved the point.

Maire ni Raighbheartaigh was a pleasant woman. He hoped she wasn't trying to 'help' him. That's the last thing he needed; charity from a bunch of overly-solicitous society women. He was content to be alone, in control.

With an Indian summer lifting spirits generally, the Northern Ireland Broadcasting Union hosted a forum on the topic 'Uniting Ireland' in its Belfast studios.

MPs, councillors, party representatives and the general public were summoned to discuss the pressing issues, live on air:

* How do we protect the Unionist inheritance and aspirations?
* What about the *catholic* Irish who vote for the Union?
* Should we work together towards a new Ireland?

* Will Europe determine our future, whether we like it or not?

There would be coffee and sandwiches afterwards.

The early contributions were a recitation of the predictable bromides. This was going nowhere. Nobody wanted to offend.

Then came the 'Movement' representative, invited due to their promise to shed new light on an old problem. Their speaker was Robert McAdam, a college lecturer. Nobody knew anything about them. He had asked for permission to include some visuals with his presentation.

A bald man of small stature, he took his place at the lectern. "Northern Ireland is dead." He paused. "It no longer exists as a viable political entity, and what remains is not worth sustaining." His audience mumbled, perhaps assuming his opening remarks were for effect and would take on a more conciliatory tone.

"Why is it dead? Because it's time is up. It is unwanted and unloved, it is a complete irrelevance to young people, it is a bar to progress on this island, and is an embarrassment to the mainland of Britain. It is a sinking ship and, like the Titanic, those who try to stick with it are like those fiddlers on the deck who went down with their ship singing Abide With Me."

A member of parliament seated at the top table voiced his offence and asked the rapporteur Damien Devenney to intervene.

"I will not try to pull the wool over your eyes; you have to realise that your position is hopeless and you have to jump ship while you still can."

Cries of 'Rubbish', whoops of approval.

"I am a Protestant, like many here, but I have witnessed the tender mercies and muddling of Britain when we called for help. So where do we go from here?

"If nothing else, I'd like you to take home from here today a little phrase to help you come to terms with the future." He aimed the remote control and these words appeared on the screen:

'We are Ireland. Ireland is Us'

"This is very simple, people. We are Ireland, Ireland is us. What does that mean? It means that we, all of us, in this room, are the sovereign power on the island of Ireland. We *own* this island, and the island in turn, is our identity. Belfast is ours; we own Belfast. Derry is ours; we own Derry. And have no doubt, Dublin is ours, and we are Dublin.

"So, if you are on a sinking ship, or you are uncertain as to where your loyalty lies, and you want somewhere to go, you can have Dublin, for that is ours. A reverse take-over, if you like.

"And we in The Movement can help you get it. It's your island; first, take it, and then you can determine your relationships with other countries."

He now had the audience's full attention.

"Now, there is a price to pay for this. And goodness knows many people in Northern Ireland have already paid a great price. The forced partition of this island has been a disaster, for both sides. This partition has to end, now. And the price is this…" he pressed the remote again;

'I AFFIRM MY ALLEGIANCE TO IRELAND'

"There's the deal. You only have to affirm your allegiance to Ireland. Not Dublin, not Northern Ireland, not London, not Europe. Ireland! What has gone before is over. It's your island; take it… or leave it."

Pressing the remote again, he stepped down without taking questions, leaving the words THE MOVEMENT and a flag billowing on the screen; a flag with the image of a black raven in flight imposed on a four-pointed white star on a green background.

Having resolved to go to Sligo, he was relieved that the engagement with the string quartet came before his debut at Galway. It would be a chance to practice dealing with the world again. His work at the shop allowed him to be polite, obliging and retiring. He found that customers were willing to deal with him on those terms. One young man had asked for a copy of '*Broken Vows*', an account of the atrocities of the IRA since the Good Friday agreement, written by a Dublin journalist and in which The Druid and O'Toole had featured prominently, with photographs.

O'Toole served the customer from behind his reading glasses and kept his composure, aware the youth could be a media plant. He volunteered he was studying Modern Irish History at UCD. Had the shop assistant read the book? No, but the author was a well-regarded student of Irish affairs and the publishers were a major British imprint, so would have checked their sources. The book would probably be a useful contribution to his studies. The youth was pleased and departed.

The drive to Sligo on a fresh early October evening was pleasant and unhurried, given the considerable burden of history that accompanies that route. As he had promised himself an evening's immersion in the quieter Ireland west of the Shannon, he had found a suitable music CD in the shop with Emmet Spiceland, The Johnstons, Tommy Makem, Willie Clancy and others; a collection of old ballads and tunes, sweet and well rendered.

> 'Oh then fare thee well sweet Donegal, the Rosses and Gweedore,'
> - and Mullaghmore and Drumcliff and Sligo town as well.

He realised the music had been knocked out of him over the past year.

He arrived at the Arena in good form. In the car park, he stayed in the car for a few minutes to see how people were dressed. His reconnoitre convinced him to put on a tie.

She would look to see if he was there, of course, so he sat in the middle of the middle row so as not to give the impression of acting strangely. On one side, an elderly woman and her daughter, a homely woman with no wedding ring. On his right, a middle-aged matron who made notes in her programme margins.

The evening was introduced by Proinsias O'Maolchraoibhe, leader of the National Symphony. The audience was, as was the programme, restrained and studied, and at half-time, proceeded in an ordered and deferential fashion to the back where refreshments were available. O'Toole noticed that the Quartet remained in place and discussed parts of the program energetically. Maire ni Raighbheartaigh looked fetching, he thought, in her flowing ensemble.

The evening concluded with Vivaldi's 'Autumn' from The Four Seasons. Mellow now, but a harbinger of winter. Bundoran would be wild. He looked forward to the coffee bar being set up in the shop so people could stay and read at leisure when the cold and the winter gales came.

He moved to the foyer in order to convenience M. ni R. in case she wished to talk to him. She would surely be engaged by other concert-goers. He held on to the programme so he would have something to do with his hands and would not look awkward.

The note-maker passed by, expressing reservations to her friend as to whether the tempo of some of the pieces truly reflected the composer's state of depression at the time they were composed.

The Quartet obviously enjoyed each other's company as they entertained their admirers in a wide circle. O'Toole would not stay too long; he did not want to look like a 'stage-door-Johnny'. Fortunately, she came from the bar and greeted him with "How did we do?"

O'Toole admitted "I thought you were very good."

"Not a bit fussy in places, did you think?"

"I wouldn't be competent to comment on that."

"You're very diplomatic. But thank you for coming. Nice to see you. You didn't need the other ticket…?"

"No, but I did enjoy the concert nevertheless."

Well, that was fairly clear. She wished him safe home and "see you again." She was going to the hotel with friends for a late bite. A satisfactory outing, overall.

On the way home, he was disposed to think of life in a more positive way. Music was a drug and M. ni R. was charming. He'd leave it at that for the time being, and not project anything.

The Atlantic drive is lovely, of course. The stark outline of Classiebawn Castle stirred in him some regret at the demise of the 'Big House'. It took him back a few years to his hunting days and the glorious careering over the Guinness lands at Leixlip.

This pleasant memory was cut off when he was seized by concern over what he would say at this Galway parade. Since his life had been fractured over his joust with The Druid and his subsequent exile in Belize, the cage in which he had locked himself permitted no reflections on politics or much else; only survival. He had no idea what he believed anymore, if anything. He'd have to go back to his university days when he believed something, though he could hardly remember what that was.

And showing up on a stage in Galway! These people were political. They'd know him and know his record. There might even be police colleagues from Dublin in the crowd. Why did he accept the invitation from DD in the first place? Well, it wasn't really an invitation. More a command. Calling in a favour based on an old friendship. How long did he know her? Good God, from 1991. And he'd never questioned her friendship even when she got him involved with The Druid, a ruthless zealot, incarcerated for conspiracy to murder.

In his heightened state of mind, he now thought about *who* DD might be. A friendly woman certainly. Pretty, lively. It was part of her charm. Nice family, good job, moral, professional. And as they were friends, he had never accorded her any agenda which was different from his own. She wouldn't risk everything to pursue a hazardous political course, would she? And if she would, where would that leave him in the piece?

He could always pull out, leave the job she got him in the bookshop, so he would owe her nothing. That's if he believed in nothing.

For the rest of the journey home, he tried to think of what he did believe in. He was sure of only one thing; the surge of resentment he felt when the British bombed the research ship Cupp on the Thames during negotiations with the British Prime Minister. Was that feeling one of patriotism, or just resentment?

And the letter. He had never opened the letter entrusted to him by The Druid. But he knew what was in it. DD did too.

If O'Toole threw himself into the speech, what had gone before wouldn't matter. But this would assuredly position him within the machinery of revolution. He would become a public figure again. He had to be prepared to live a new life. On one hand, he had nothing else; on the other, it would mark him out, giving rise to issues of personal security. For this 'Movement', he was sure, could not exist entirely peacefully. The bookshop would become a focal point for activists, from all sides.

CHAPTER 2

Senator Oliver d'Arcy came of a wealthy Protestant family. His people had been English Huguenot gentry whose gift-of-conquest lands in fertile County Meath had provided corn and cattle to British naval forces on the India route during the *Gorta Mór*, the Great Famine in Ireland.

Under the protection of the British Crown, his family had prospered up until 1921 when the ousting of British rule and the establishment of the Irish Free State had forced them to practice 'becoming Irish' to survive.

Keeping a careful balance during the Irish Civil War of 1922/23 prevented their 'big house' from being burned, but they finally had to take sides and opt for either Michael Collins or Eamon De Valera. In 1923, Dan d'Arcy, the patriarch of the family, had publicly thrown his hat in with Cumann na nGaedheal/Fine Gael, the pro-Free State party, and thus was on the side of the governing party for the first nine years of the new state.

His donations to the defeated De Valera and his Fianna Fail party were more private, but essential to longevity for all that. In 1933, his son Ted ran for parliament and was elected with a greater number of votes than the natural Fine Gael majority in the constituency. Old Dan was vindicated.

In politics, a number of sins are mitigated by being a good constituency MP. Ted minded his people, was prominent at births, marriages and funerals, kept the farmers happy, and made sure he knew which way people were voting before they voted.

After thirty years as a TD (*Teachta Dail*; member of parliament, Irish Republic), he handed the job on a plate to his son Oliver who continued the family tradition and thrived through schism and coup and eventually became Minister for Agriculture.

As farmers are perpetually poor – even the rich ones – he had to be seen to fight for funds in Dublin and Europe on all possible occasions. That he coincidentally enriched himself in the process was marked down as a perk of his exalted position. As old Dan had ordained, he was always careful to share his good fortune with his constituents.

In time, he became Oliver *senior* as along came Oliver *junior* who in turn felt obliged to accept the family sinecure of the parliamentary seat following a spell in the Irish Army. There was a wobble in the dynasty in the late 1980s when he lost in a by-election to a Local Hospital candidate, but he gathered himself, proffered some funds to the hospital and the natural order was restored in the next election.

Many years later, now Father of The House, he had little more to achieve except groom his daughter Alanna for the job (for it was the Time of Women) and keep a paternal eye on the big picture. To facilitate the family's dynastic progression, he resigned his seat mid-term (for health reasons), was kicked upstairs to the Senate (by arrangement with the Taoiseach), and ensured Alanna's success in the subsequent by-election.

Two days after The Movement parade in Galway, the Connacht Recorder carried this article:

> 'A parade by a hitherto unknown group, 'The Movement', took place in Galway on Sunday. About 500 people assembled at Salthill with their numbers swelled by others, mainly students, along the route to Eyre Square.
>
> It was an orderly and jolly affair, led by a flute band and some very colourful banners carried by young men and women. The age range of the participants was from 5 to 80. Following speeches in Eyre Square, the public was entertained by a Ceili band and some other well-known musicians.
>
> It was not immediately clear at the outset of the parade what were the aims or purposes of *The Movement*. Many marchers carried flags proclaiming 'We are Ireland ~ Ireland is us'. It is hard to argue with that.
>
> Of particular interest was the appearance throughout the parade of several very large, expensive 'siege' banners (these

banners were 7 feet long and 5 or 6 feet wide, supported on stout poles, and are of the type often seen at Orangemen's marches or the Miners' Gala in Durham) and flags depicting a white 4-pointed star on a green background and imposed on the star, a black crow or raven in flight. It must be said this was a very striking image. Many of the marchers were sporting a button brooch or stick-on image of this flag.

This was certainly intriguing, and this reporter and others were anxious to get an explanation of the march. (Apparently invitations to attend the event had been sent by snail-mail to all registered news franchises in Britain and Ireland). A steward wearing a jacket with 'Steward' helpfully printed on front and back directed me to a horse-trailer labelled 'Media Centre'.

There we were greeted by Mrs. Doreen Downey from Derry who described herself as Public Relations officer for *The Movement*. In the horsebox were a number of walkie-talkies in a charger array, a good number of flags and banners, and a plastic bin full of the button brooches noted earlier. Several laptop screens displayed live images from along the proposed route.

We were each given a Media pack, which was welcome and evidenced a degree of planning and resources. I moved to the side to study this information, passing as I did a large photograph on a tripod of five smiling boys and girls unfurling the 'Raven' flag outside a building which looked very much like Dail Eireann.

As I read the literature, I was forced to divert from all the sweetness and light which had attended my initial experience of the gathering as I read their Declaration of Aims which I reproduce here verbatim:

'**A house divided cannot stand.** For 100 years now, this island has been unnaturally divided in two with a group of Unionists/Loyalists in the Six Counties giving their allegiance to another country. THIS HAS TO STOP.

In perpetuating this divide, they have caused strife, pain and stultifying suspicion. They have stunted the progress of this island and are an international embarrassment. They are loathed in London, laughed at in Europe and dismissed in America for the pariah they are.

They are recognised only for their sullen countenance and entrenched bigotry. They are antiques. Their time is up.

'**The Movement** is a spontaneous reaction by the forward-looking in Ireland to the outdated and irrelevant nostrums of the past.

It is our **objective** to reclaim this island and position it for a harmonious, civilised future that will harness and develop the natural genius of the indomitable Irish, a genius that is recognised and admired throughout the world.

In order to achieve this future, ALL citizens of this island must henceforth confirm their allegiance to ONE NATION.

~ If you do not like that nation… it's yours; we will change it together.

~ If you don't like *that*, you are welcome to go elsewhere.

Galway is ours, Dublin is ours, Belfast is ours, Cork and Derry are ours. And WE are Ireland.

'We will carry out a series of parades and carnivals to celebrate ourselves and our country. All are welcome to join these festivities. We will acknowledge the past but look to the future.

Immediate evidence of this is in the new flag under which we march; the **green** of Ireland for which we are known and which is worn by our international representatives with pride; the four-pointed **star** to recognise the four provinces of Ireland; and the **raven**, the symbol of sovereignty and rebirth.

'It does not matter which political party or football team you support, what religion you are, what language you speak or aspire to. As long as you support the single objective of

The Movement, you are one of us. AND WE ARE IRELAND.

Now, on with the celebrations…'

On the front of the press pack, there was a running order for the day's activities. Speeches to begin at 3pm. As it was now 2pm, this reporter moved smartly with the rearguard of the parade to reach Eyre Square in good time.

The parade moved in small groups rather than as a formal march, so people could vary their speed and join different friends as and when they met, rather like a crowd going to a sporting fixture.

At Eyre Square, the crowd seemed to number well over 1500. The organisers would be satisfied with their initial outing. A large flat-bed lorry bearing flags, chairs and microphones acted as the stage. While awaiting the speakers, we were well entertained by the pleasant playing of the Dublin Mozart Ensemble followed by renderings of *To Ramona* and *Wide Open Spaces* by that fine Limerick singer Eileen ni Doibhilin.

There followed two speeches noteworthy for different reasons:

The Keynote speech was given by Mr. Robert McAdam from Belfast. His is a name that was new to me, but when details of his biography were circulated, it transpires that he comes from very distinguished lines in that his great grand-uncle, Robert Shipboy MacAdam (1808–1895), was a Belfast Presbyterian, educated at Royal Belfast Academical Institution, an industrialist, antiquarian and Gaelic scholar. He was one of the founders of the Botanic Gardens. He was the first librarian of Queen's College in Belfast, a member of the Irish Harp Society, and his invaluable collection of Irish language manuscripts are now held in Belfast Central Library.

His namesake might admit to more modest accomplishments. 45 year old Mr. Robert McAdam is a lecturer in computer studies at Belfast Polytechnic. I am not aware that he has had any previous involvement in politics, but he was introduced as a Founding Director of *The Movement*.

Mr. McAdam reiterated the Aims & Objects of *The Movement* as noted above. Some of his listeners might have been marked down as 'rent-a-crowd' because I saw familiar faces from the old Civil Rights days, but there were many young people who seemed to enjoy the festivities and were able to relate to the forward-looking agenda.

The second speaker was a very interesting figure indeed; Ex-Garda Detective Inspector Turlough O'Toole will be well known to many readers. He resigned (or was drummed out of) the Garda Siochana at a Special Tribunal two years ago for dereliction of duty and bringing the Force into disrepute during the infamous 'Druid' case. He then quit the jurisdiction, but apparently has returned and now works in a bookshop in Co. Donegal.

I am not privy to Mr. O'Toole's politics prior to his leaving the Gardai, but it seems quite a leap from being a Guardian of the Peace to advocate for the radical displacement of a significant part of the population of Northern Ireland.

Mr. O'Toole's contribution was based on the relatively safe ground of *Hope, Confidence and Imagination*, attributes of the Irish notably addressed by President John Fitzgerald Kennedy while on his triumphal progress through the Republic in June 1963.

There was no evidence of dissent from the meeting which broke up in good order and in good spirits at about 5.30pm. Organisers pronounced the event a success and announced a more substantial event in Dublin two weeks hence.'

Driving up to Dublin for a sitting of the Upper House on Tuesday morning, Senator d'Arcy was uneasy. If it had been an ordinary constituency matter, that would be easily resolved. If it had been the Opposition being difficult, that would allow him to make an amusing and conciliatory speech in the *Seanad* and thus enhance his reputation as the *eminence grise* of the parliament. A national treasure. As long as events were under control.

But this was more problematic. He had read the article in the Connacht Recorder and could foresee difficulty. This crowd were going on a series of marches, they were non-party-political, but they were looking for a United Ireland. That was all very well; it was an aspiration in the Constitution, and we already had Sinn Fein as a declared Republican party. But we had them under control to some extent, within the democratic process; they had parliamentary representatives, they knew the rules of the game.

This new crowd were a populist outfit, a loose cannon. They want to 'Reclaim the Island'! What in God's name does that mean? And *all* must give allegiance to Ireland. Where does that leave Unionists in the North? And in the South? We've had a hundred years now playing with our republic; we don't want a million Unionists coming down here and screwing up a good thing. The bloody place would end up like a bigger version of Northern Ireland!

Maybe they'll disappear. Reports say eight hundred at Galway; nothing to worry about there, yet. But Dublin might be different. There's a lot of agitation, fluid thinking, young activists, Europe. And Sinn Fein have annoyed the Old School with their flakey social policies.

D'Arcy's people had always re-invented themselves when survival was called for. He'd keep a watching brief.

It was now four months since the plane had released enhanced Anthrax over Chipping Norton in England, and the town was a wasteland. Surrounded completely for a radius of three miles by electrified fences and army units, everything was closed, all civilians gone, all animals incinerated. The work to encase surfaces in formaldehyde was continuing; it would take two years. Off-colour jokes in the pub described it as the 'dead centre of England'.

Not far off the mark. The short-term death toll was one hundred and ninety two. There was a silence over the Home Counties of England. It had never been like this, even during the war.

The failure to find other locations where Anthrax might be hidden, ready to be used by accident or on purpose, left the population on edge. Small aircraft movements restricted, except military. Many people had stopped buying aerosols, just in case. Endless disruption. The Scottish parliament didn't want any more incinerations on its islands. Isle of Man? Channel Islands? Northern Ireland? Space?

Gerald Ashton was in office four months. He had to be careful; he knew high office was lost more often by accident than by design. Some women would be nearly four months pregnant now. That's what bothered him; women becoming pregnant after the plane had sprayed, but *before* the government told them that this bug was different, engineered, so that it could be transmitted by sex, *white on white* sex.

"*We will breed ourselves to death,*" the scientists said. What would the babies be if they went to term? The word was we'll have to force abortions!

During the week, O'Toole had fielded questions and observations on his contribution at Galway. He was reasonably prepared, saying that he had been asked to speak on 'being Irish', but a number of customers had replied that the object of The Movement seemed to be something more pointed that that. Possibly, he agreed, though he hadn't signed up for any particular ideology or political viewpoint; just 'being Irish'.

Most acquiesced, but Captain Butchart-Grimley, ex-British army and now a steward at the Galway Races, admonished him to 'thread carefully' while paying for his copy of the latest Man Booker prize-winner.

O'Toole contented himself that most people were commenting on his participation in the event rather than on The Movement itself which many considered to be a self-help organisation, the likes of which had risen and fallen in various manifestations over the years, particularly west of the Shannon.

On Friday morning, he received a call on his mobile from DD. "What's the feedback like?" As DD immersed herself more and more in political activity, so O'Toole was conscious of getting more remote from her.

"Not bad, in general."

"You did well. Faith and Motherhood, but that's fine; it bears repeating. You're off the hook now for a while. You won't be speaking in Dublin next week. But listen, be sure to be there, we have a very special guest appearing."

"Well, that's interesting. Are you expecting a big crowd?"

"Indeed we are. Bigger than Galway. As you know, we've been getting some column-inches in the papers, and we'll be building on that. And we're doing a push on social media. For the first time in Irish history, we're a radical group which is well financed and has a plan. Our next parade after the winter will be an extravaganza in Belfast in the spring. There will be a lot of work going into it, and a lot of PR and social media and radio. We have to get a critical mass of Unionists, North and South, to empathise if not actually join us. That's the exercise for the winter."

"Great. Is there anything you want me to do for next week?"

"Can you take a car load of people with you? You can all meet up in Bundoran. Actually, the bookshop is a good rendezvous."

"That's fine."

He returned to his paid duties and spent the afternoon with Daithi dressing the windows with a selection of works appropriate to the Celtic festival of Samhain. They set up a kiddie's corner labelled 'Halloween', featuring druids, wood nymphs and Ogham swirls.

It occurred to him it was exactly two years since he had set out upon his path to perdition with his meeting with The Druid at the Hell Fire Club. And now here was DD again, summoning him back to a world that had been his downfall.

Saturday mornings were always pleasant at the shop. People were relaxed, unhurried, chatty. There were football games to attend, dinners to be planned, gardens to be raked, books to be read.

So he was in a benign frame of mind when Maire ni Raighbheartaigh appeared. She knew his mobile number but had not phoned about his participation in Galway. She undoubtedly knew about it. Did she disapprove, or was she sparing him the embarrassment? Or did she just have nothing to say? She was a bright, sophisticated woman, so it was unlikely to be the latter. He was pleased to greet her with a smile.

She approached boldly and said without preamble "Toby, I want you to do two things for me." As his usual mode of interaction with her was one of deference, he stumbled. She had never called him Toby before.

"Wha... yes?"

"First, I want you to call me Maire. And second, I want you to come riding with us. Tomorrow afternoon, at Rossnowlagh. We're having a picnic. Kathleen is bringing Tommy Mallin and you're bringing me. We have all the gear and there are no political meetings tomorrow, so you're in the clear."

When a defensive, isolated and traumatised man receives an unsolicited invitation from an admired source, it results in serious difficulty. A man who has a low opinion of himself questions why he should receive such an invitation. An unworthy thought perhaps. Then his defences rise and he is likely to be rash and ungallant in replying. He is likely to say 'no' and risks offending his host. He had no idea who Tommy Mallin was.

O'Toole stared at Maire and for a moment fought the urge to decline with profuse thanks and go back to his solitary, safe, satisfactory existence. There was no attitude of patronage in her demeanour that he could judge. As he delayed his answer, the edges of her eyes creased slightly suggesting she had invested considerably in the initiative and his answer was a matter of importance. "I would be pleased to do both."

The former editor of the Cotswold Examiner, now diseased, tottered to the window of his quarantine block. He tried to see his wife and surviving child one hundred miles away in the concentration camp at Stamford army range in East Anglia. He could see only to the high wall surrounding Imber sixty feet away.

Supporting himself by the end of the bed, he retraced the path to the whisky bottle and slumped down. The sores on his arms were bruised, black and festered. They said he was lucky; few were surviving this attack. He looked for the luck. It was there, all right, and it was all bad.

Seventy miles to the north, his home was drenched in formaldehyde. They said the land could not be used again for fifty years. That meant not in his lifetime.

They were afraid he'd have sex with his wife, so they separated them. He had heard rumours; all babies from Chipping Norton being forcibly aborted, incinerated. For months, he had cried over his little Helen. They put her in a steel box. They wouldn't let him see her. Now he sees her all the time.

He had always been a rational man, a resourceful man. Now he was a shell of a man with dry eyes.

CHAPTER 3

It was a long time since Turlough O'Toole was prepared to consider happiness, so he would not think about it too much.

To the music of Hank Snow, he fished out his jodhpurs and brushed the dust off. His riding boots hadn't survived his dispirited retreat from society, but Tommy Mallin would lend him a pair at the beach. His hunting jacket, which he had bought in Maynooth all those years ago, was still in good condition.

It's funny, he thought, of all the things he could have saved when his life was at a low ebb, he had held on to his riding jacket and the statuette of the dying hero Cú Chullain. Strange. The riding jacket, when he was at his happiest; Cú Chullain? Hope in the midst of woe.

He was pleased. He felt vindicated. There was hope. His strength was returning. He would lead a life in the background where his strength was adequate and where he would not face extraordinary demands. His life as a book-seller was good; friendly, solicitous people, intellectual satisfaction, enough money to live on, a credible, and respectable, member of society. He could not allow DD to encroach too much.

The bell rang. Looking out the window, his face lit up. A horsebox!

He collected the items he had carefully assembled for a quick exit – jodhpurs, jacket, crop, riding hat (new), cheese and wine for the picnic – and descended to meet his new friends.

Climbing the step to the passenger seat, he was greeted by Maire from the living area behind. "Toby. Nice to have you with us. This is Tommy Mallin, chauffeur and gentleman farmer, and Kathleen you know." He set his burden down on the bench seat and stretched to meet the hand of Tommy Mallin, a comfortable-looking chap of forty-ish with a broad, open smile.

"Good man Toby. Are you in?"

"Hello Toby. Nice to see you again." He recognised Kathleen from the String Quartet which had played in Sligo the week before. She and Maire were holding drinks. Maire was nursing a bottle of whiskey with an open picnic basket at her feet. She offered Toby a sandwich as he sorted himself out in front and Tommy nosed the lorry up the quiet street. "What's your poison?"

"It's very early in the day, but maybe a very small whiskey?" He knew anything more would turn him on his ear given his state of excitement. Maire handed him his request in return for which he sent back the wine and cheese.

"Maire tells me you're a great horseman," said Tommy.

"Oh God, I am not. Haven't been on a horse for two years, and last time I was on I fell off!"

"No.,. How?"

So O'Toole related his adventures two years before at the St. Stephen's Day hunt at Shillelagh in the County Wicklow when he broke a leg landing after a hedge.

"And are you better now?"

"I hope so. On a nice, quiet horse."

"We've got the very girl for you. Come and meet Beanie." O'Toole climbed over the seat and into the Living. Maire and Kathleen were on their feet and opened the jockey door to where the three horses were stalled. He was assaulted by the sweet acid smell of horse urine. Nearest was a plain horse of 16.3 hands who regarded him with a big full eye. "That's Beanie."

He hadn't touched a horse for so long. He placed a palm on her neck and rested it there, waiting for the movement, the heat and the spirit of the horse to transmit to his starved soul. The two women stood back and watched. They gave him his moment of resurrection. A part of his mind that had been suspended behind a locked door opened and a quiet, soft light descended. For a moment he felt unbalanced. "Aren't you a lovely horse!" He turned to face his friends. "There's only three horses?"

"Yes. We're having a relay system. As Kathleen is a bit of a wimp, she's only having a short ride with me grounded, then I'll take over. You two boys can go off and do manly things. I'll catch up."

"Isn't she an awful blather?" said Tommy. "We'll take it nice and easy at the start. They say you're a ferocious jockey…?" Tommy Mallin was a farmer. Sheep in this part of the country. He and his father before him kept a few horses for breeding and racing. Tommy was a noted amateur jockey in the Point-to-Point field, so would be no slouch going over the sand dunes at Rossnowlagh. O'Toole was relieved to hear they'd take it easy at the start; these horsey farmers tend to be tough, hell-for-leather lads in the saddle, the bold Irish horseman. O'Toole had seen them (out-jumping him) often enough in the hunting field.

With a light breeze and compact sand, the strand was ideal for the horse. Getting on was a giggle. O'Toole's mare Beanie was quiet enough, but went walkies every time he placed a foot in the stirrup to mount up. So there he was, hanging over the side as Beanie ambled up the beach and Tommy Mallin shouting "Are you going to get on?" The bookseller abandoned ship and led the horse back to the lorry and remounted the steps while Maire held the horse's head. Success!

Kathleen had a smaller horse, a nice little Connemara/thoroughbred cross which she mounted unassisted and with some grace. O'Toole suspected she mightn't be as much of a wimp as suggested earlier. With three riders mounted, Maire produced a hip flask and they each had a nip 'to keep out the Atlantic breeze'. She wished them Happy Trails and set about clearing the beach of droppings.

A big mottled sky, clement for the time of year, opened ahead of them. O'Toole was prepared for his horse dancing with excitement, as was often the case at the beginning of the hunt, but Beanie and her two companions were quite sedate. They'd been here before.

Kathleen and Tommy were lively and did not talk shop. They asked O'Toole about his adventures in the hunting field and his work in the bookshop. He admitted he was content and glad of the company after a period of being 'not that well'. There was talk of horses, the forthcoming P-to-P season, and music. Kathleen played Oboe in the National Symphony and happened to live fairly near Maire. O'Toole did enjoy classical and expressed his liking for Rachmaninoff. Kathleen and Tommy had been 'stepping out' for three years. "She's trying to knock the rough edges off me. She makes me go to these concerts so I'll be fit for civilised society."

"Now who's the blather?" said Kathleen.

Tommy proposed a canter as they had now turned and a mile away the outline of the lorry could be seen. O'Toole shortened his reins and edged in behind Tommy in case his horse made an unwarranted charge. He would know soon if Beanie had brakes.

Beanie moved on smartly and O'Toole found himself flying smoothly as the breeze ripped past his ears. Kathleen moved upsides from the rear and matched him yard for yard, giving him some confidence. Tommy was keeping a steady pace upfront and O'Toole felt himself adjust to a very ancient rhythm, a man in control of a cantering horse. There is nothing more divine.

Kathleen was out of the saddle, on a short rein, but he saw her fingers playing the bit and her horse changing stride and outline in sympathy. A well-collected horse. Fine riding. She smiled over at him. "Want to go?"

"Will you go with me?"

"I will."

In a fit of exuberance, he pulled his horse to the right and kicked, and the big hunter and the little Connemara charged down the strand. O'Toole fixed his knees tight to the saddle and realised in his excitement he was scrubbing, kneading the neck with the heels of his fists in time to the up and down of the horse's head. Man as centaur. Kathleen was with him. "Can you stop?" she cried.

"Aggh! Don't know."

They flashed past either side of the lorry and O'Toole took a pull. Legs off, heels down, steady back on the reins. "Whoa, whoa." Beanie came back, with a disconcerting shaking of her head, anxious to drive on. Blessed is the rider whose horse comes to hand after a charge. He bounced proudly in the saddle as Beanie came to trot and turned towards the lorry to be greeted by a grinning Maire. "Glad to be back?"

"Wonderful! Sorry for galloping your horse. Sort of lost the run of myself."

"No harm done. A nice pipe-opener for Beanie. Will you walk her for a minute, then we'll hack on again?"

O'Toole circled the mare and had another nip (against the Atlantic breeze) as Maire mounted the Connemara. Kathleen and Tommy applauded him. "Good man. It's like falling off a bike, isn't it. You never forget."

"Great fun." He and Maire sauntered down the beach, exultant in the glories of Donegal.

By Wednesday, and fortified by several coffees by eleven a.m., O'Toole's thoughts had been grounded and he took to considering the parade in Dublin this coming Sunday.

There really was no reason for him to go at all; he was not speaking, he had no deep convictions on The Movement one way or the other, and any obligation he was feeling towards DD was diminished in proportion to the degree he felt himself used.

Maire was an interesting quantity, but she had made no references to his recent political activity, confining her intrusions to an invitation to brunch at the Beach Hotel on Saturday which he had to decline in favour of work. She was going to Dublin on Saturday afternoon for a week's engagement with the orchestra as they finalised their programme for the Christmas series at the National Concert Hall.

The existence of *the* letter was a consideration. At any time, an incident, an outrage, a repercussion could provide the impetus for him to give the letter to the Gardai and have done with it. But he must also think how that would play with DD's people, whoever her 'people' were.

He was put on the spot at two o'clock when he received a call from a Feargal Morrisey seeking to confirm his lift to Dublin on Sunday.

His companions for the trip to Dublin were an average band. O'Toole got the impression they were aware he was an ex-detective and so were guarded in their enthusiasm and comments. For his part, he hoped to leave an impression of even-handedness. Each had agreed to contribute ten Euros towards fuel.

As it was N3 all the way, he allowed four hours for the drive, including a fifteen minute break at Cavan. There was no game at Croke Park that day but there was racing at Navan. There was more of a chance of running into that traffic on the return journey.

O'Toole wasn't sure if he could trust himself to remain sociable all the way, but arriving at Phibsborough in North Dublin he found himself to be indeed even-handed in his mind and well disposed to making arrangements for the return trip. They went their separate ways. "Have a good day, Toby. See you later."

He was now on his old stomping ground and briefly considered a pint at The Quare Fellow but the risk of running into ex-Gardai was too great so he went to a fast food café instead from where he could watch the parade assemble in safety.

And he had another errand. This was the closest he had been to her flat in two years. From where he was sitting, he could see the smokestack of the Mater hospital. Last time he saw that, he was looking out the window through her lace curtains; life was wonderful; it was a bright, fresh day, she was lovely, and they were just about to leave for that weekend in Connemara which started so well. He was a complete man, with the love of his life.

Then it all went wrong. All the way from Bundoran he had promised himself; he wouldn't do this. But he was here now. He had no choice. He finished his coffee quickly and went outside to find a distraction.

Several groups of entertainers were sorting themselves out. They would accompany the parade down Phibsborough Road on the route through Dame Street and College Green.

A giant Raven banner, like the one he had seen at Galway, was supported by six young people in white shirt and dark pants, and each with a glittering green cape fastened with a Tara brooch at the neck. The banner made its way to the centre of the crowd so that it was surrounded by revellers rather than leading them. The intent was obvious; to portray The Movement as an inclusive, non-threatening example of modern Ireland in contrast to the intense, fearful Civil Rights marches he had joined in his young day.

People on the sidewalks gazed at the banner, intrigued. It certainly was a striking image. Few knew what it was about, but they'd remember it. They were happy enough to make their contribution when confronted by a collection can and presented with a stick-on image of the flag and bearing the simple assertion 'We Are Ireland'.

Along the route, stewards in hi-vis jackets maintained an air of goodwill and proprietorship – the people of Ireland walking their own land without fear or apology.

O'Toole knew this was all practice for the big Belfast march. The South might regard The Movement with bemused indifference, at this early stage, but in Belfast it would be seen for what it was – a threat, a nationalist coup, a takeover.

The British would be nonplussed, and secretly hoping it would succeed. Most Unionists would be suspicious of this youth-driven pageant. They had seen the raven fluttering in an ill wind on the town hall at Cookstown; a sign of what was to come.

Detective Garda Mick Devlin was an OK cop. He wasn't going to be a great cop. He had no interest in socialising with the big knobs. He was interested in football. However, bills to pay, a new wife to support and season tickets to buy for Dalymount and Croke Park. And the job was interesting enough.

Since moving to Detectives three years ago, he had done enough to keep the bossman off his tail. The only real blemish on his career was his time with Detective Inspector Turlough O'Toole. The Druid case. He had been in the media for all the wrong reasons and had barely escaped without censure at the Tribunal of Enquiry. He didn't need the heat. He was happy enough just occasionally detecting bad people and joshing with the lads at Harcourt Street station.

He didn't really want the overtime today, but it was a short shift and double time did have its attractions. He was sitting at the corner of Constitution Hill and Western Way looking not very inconspicuous in an unmarked car. People in the parade would nod while passing; "Hiya Gard". It was all good humoured.

He had the news on the car radio. The parade got a mention - on the traffic report. He was a bit surprised at the number of young people in the parade. Something must have got them motivated. He had promised the missus dinner out in return for being missing most of the day.

He was not thinking of ex-detective Toby O'Toole when he first saw him in the middle of the parade, hands in pockets, exchanging pleasantries with another middle-aged man walking beside him. But it was certainly him! The last he'd heard, O'Toole had left the country following his resignation after the Tribunal. They let him resign rather than be fired. They knew he was leaving the country.

But here he was, large as life. What in God's name was he doing back in the country? Devlin was tempted to jump out of the car and hail him. But the complications... He slumped down in the seat as much as possible. O'Toole passed.

The best thing to do was follow the parade down to O'Connell Street and keep an eye from there. He radioed base he was moving.

Lower O'Connell Street was packed. A forty-foot flatbed truck was set up opposite the GPO with Raven flags slotted at six feet intervals on the flatbed (political parades always tended to assemble at the General Post Office in order to claim legitimacy and respectability from the fallen of the 1916 revolution who had commandeered the post office as a base) and a *céilí* band on the lorry was belting out The Waves of Tory, a tune he recognised from his childhood when his parents had packed him off to the *Gaeltacht*, the Irish-speaking area of Donegal, to learn his native language and so honour his forefathers. He remembered shuffling his stringy body in embarrassed disarray as Miss Minnie thumped out the tunes on the piano.

In their Irish dancing costumes, a group of well-schooled boys and girls now floated and stepped, emulating the waves of the sea.

Devlin flashed his badge and parked in blocked-off Cathedral Street where huddles of uniformed Gardai lolled and chatted, keeping a low profile. "There won't be any trouble from this lot." The crowd swayed, laughed and applauded.

As Devlin edged forward, a cheer went up. Then a clear, unadorned voice:

> 'If you ever go across the sea to Ireland,
> Then maybe at the closing of your day
> You can sit and watch the moon rise over Claddagh
> (and here the crowd joined in lustily)
> And watch the sun go down on Galway Bay.

The dancers now formed a half-moon around the singer and commenced to hum in pleasing harmony:

> Just to hear again the ripple of the trout stream
> The women in the meadows making hay,
> To sit beside the turf fire in the cabin
> And watch the barefoot gossoons at their play.
>
> For the breezes blowin' 'cross the sea from Ireland
> Are perfumed by the heather as they blow.
> And the women in the uplands diggin' praties
> Speak a language that the strangers do not know.
>
> For the strangers came and tried to teach us their way.
> They scorned us just for being what we are.
> But they might as well go chasing after moon beams
> Or light a penny candle from a star.
>
> (now the crowd in full voice)
>
> And if there's going to be a life hereafter
> And somehow I'm sure there's going to be,
> I will ask my God to let me make my heaven,
> In that dear land across the Irish sea.'

It was a sentimental, American song, but a nice song, and Devlin found himself joining in.

"Good man Gerry," exclaimed the crowd.

"Up the rebels!"

Gerry gave a thumbs-up to the crowd and left the stage, along with the *céilí* band. A middle-aged, bald man in a suit, who Devlin recognised as Robert McAdam, mounted the stage and welcomed the guests and personalities and entertainers. Devlin scanned the crowd but saw no sign of O'Toole. As he was five feet ten inches, O'Toole wouldn't stand out. Being six feet one, Devlin anchored himself at the base of the 'Needle' monument (or the *Skewer* as the locals had it) to be less conspicuous. Stewards emerged from behind the lorry and began to mingle with the crowd.

"Ladies and gentlemen, welcome. And thank you to our entertainers.

"We are on a great mission. It is our destiny to reclaim this island. *All* of it. We are Ireland… and Ireland is us!" The crowd applauded, after some hesitation.

"It is said that war benefits from being fought on many fronts. We have with us today someone who has struck a great blow for Ireland." Devlin was intrigued and came alert. A sportsman? A musician? A writer? The crowd murmured. McAdam lifted his right arm to induce someone at the back to climb the steps and take the stage. In quizzical restraint, the crowd waited and waited…

From below the lorry, sheltered by the wall of the GPO, a figure in hooded anorak and jeans rose up the steps between the raven flags and took several careful steps, not towards the microphone, but to the side, all the time looking to the left so her face (for clearly it was a female) was not easily seen. The crowd waited for a cue. No words were spoken. McAdam left his microphone and walked back to shake the hand of the furtive hero. She remained obscured by the hood, but raised a clenched fist to the crowd. A statement, sewn at the front of the crowd, gradually began to seep backwards.

"Who is it? Who is it?"

"It's the pilot."

"What pilot?"

And in barely a whisper, "The Anthrax pilot."

Leaning against the plinth of the 'skewer', Devlin could only be puzzled by events which he took to be poor stage management. For the 'hero' had now left the stage without a word. A fellow in a cloth cap just in front of him whispered loudly to those near him "It's the Anthrax pilot".

Devlin startled, "The what?"

The fellow in the cloth cap placed a hand on his arm. "The Anthrax pilot, y'know, in England".

Obeying an impulse which had first propelled him into the police force, Devlin lurched forward. He wasn't going to be caught wanting like O'Toole in the face of this obscenity. He would do the honourable thing; he would do his duty!

He almost knocked down the man in the cloth cap. He was at least ten rows back from the lorry. If he called for help on his radio, he would be surrounded and felled. He pushed to get closer. People protested. He pushed further. As he stood head and shoulders above the crowd, several hi-viz stewards saw his coming. They closed. He pushed again. Nearer the lorry. Trouble. He had to call now, regardless: "Code red code red, Devlin at the GPO." Three rows from the lorry "This is Detective Garda Devlin…" He remembers falling to the ground.

Chapter 4

A small farm came up for sale near Tullyhogue in County Tyrone. It was placed with the auctioneer by the executors of the late Ross Abercrombie, a bachelor farmer who had lived in the village.

Ross was a staunch Loyalist. He marched on the Twelfth of July, attended the Apprentice Boys in Derry in December and was an active member of the Boyne Defenders Loyal Orange Lodge 109. He had always been happy to affirm Sir Basil Brooke's boast that he 'never had a Catholic about the place'.

The farm was not exceptional; an outlying twenty-five acres with a barn, suitable for animal husbandry and tillage. The gates and hedges were sound, there was piped water, and while the soil was not the best-draining in the world, it attracted considerable interest, particularly from the other small farmers locally.

Access to the land was by a short lane from the main road. At the junction with the main road was a crumbling gable wall that had originally been part of an artisan dwelling, the home of old Johnny McGovern, the cooper, who had lived a quiet nineteenth century existence with tilly lamps, a turf fire and an outside convenience.

Three weeks later, the land was sold. The buyer, a company registered in Barbados, was represented by a solicitor in Dungannon. This caused ample chatter among the population.

A week after that, two lads arrived in a tipper lorry with a load of stones, sand and scaffolding. They proceeded to repair and plaster the gable wall, then departed, leaving the scaffold. Locals mused about whether the scaffolding was holding the wall up or the wall was holding the scaffolding up.

When the plaster hardened, two different fellows arrived and commenced to paint a sign on the side of the wall facing the road. With the scaffolding removed, the sign read

'LAND HELD IN TRUST
FOR
THE O'NEILL COLLECTIVE'.

Prominent atop the sign was the red hand of the clan Ui Neill, hereditary kings of the ancient province of Ulster.

Facing the busy Stewartstown/Cookstown road as it did, this development could not be let pass and urgent enquiries were made. The solicitor couldn't, or wouldn't, shed light and, by the time a man showed up with a lorry load of horses to graze the land, the local newspapers had already been to photograph and speculate.

The horseman was a well-known breeder and huntsman and was paying his rent to the solicitor in Dungannon.

Comments began to appear on social media and the meaning of the wall became clear; the 'O'Neill Collective' was, according in informed sources, a Nationalist front and this purchase was a deliberate attempt to sweep up land hitherto in the possession of loyal protestant Planter stock deep in the heartland of Ulster.

Unionists were already smarting over the relentless increase in nationalist voting power and land claims that were proceeding at a snail's pace through the European Court of Justice in Strasbourg. Since the ruling by the Court that there was a case to be answered (based on the success of First Nations and Inuit in Canada), Unionist hard-liners had barricaded the town of Cookstown in the midst of nationalist County Tyrone, declaring it a 'Loyal Enclave'.

Nationalists had charged that the land had been usurped from them 'by force and deception', with no legal justification, and was the rightful domain of the ancient Clan O'Neill of Ulster. In the interests of advancing negotiations, the O'Neill claim would apply first to lands currently vested in the name of the British Crown; National Trust land, buildings and other assets would be ceded to the Irish equivalent.

The dispute had been running for some time now, and most regarded it as an interesting but frivolous anomaly. The nationalist plaintiffs declared that their stewardship of the land would not affect the current rights of leaseholders except that ownership of the land, at the termination of current leases, would legally be vested in The O'Neill Collective, a co-operative acting on behalf of the natural citizens of Ireland.

Unionists claimed that this was a back-door attempt at ethnic cleansing of ten generations of British Planters and settlers. In a speech in Cookstown three days later, the rabble-rousing loyalist preacher and MP, William (Billy) McKay, warned his Unionist audience "This is the thin edge of a wedge. This is the beginning of a Nationalist putsch. Unionists in mid-Ulster are being squeezed, deprived of their heritage. Be in no doubt; the real message on that wall in Tullyhogue is To Hell or to Scotland!"

McKay announced that an urgent meeting had been scheduled with the minister responsible in London.

Fonsie Sweeney sat atop the scaffolding looking down the lane towards Tullyhogue. He kept his baseball cap well pulled down over his eyes in case cops or other interested parties should pass by. He wasn't worried about his past; he had his life to live. If that queer at the British embassy, Cedric T. Wall, got himself killed, that was his problem. You could say he gave his life for Ireland. Pity he had such a miserable end, mind you. And the people of Oxfordshire; probably nice enough people, but they should keep their bloody armies out of Ireland.

I like the Brits. They're ok. Not very smart, but they're ok. Once they learn their lesson, they'll make great neighbours. In the meantime, they have what's coming to them. The Druid is right; they'll lie through their teeth and then try it on again. He lit another fag.

"Fonsie! Are ye going to sit on yer arse there all day?"

"Fuck off, I'm busy."

"Well, when you're finished playing with yourself, mix another barrow of muck!"

He wasn't feeling guilty. He'd been lucky so far, getting off that boat on the Thames, getting out of Deauville. He was a wee bit worried about his sister. If they got him, they might target her. She knows nothing. He never involved her. Just as well. If they get him, they'll never let him out. Let her marry that big drip of water Finbar; wanker cop. He won't be able to go to the wedding; it'll be wall-to-wall Gards. He'll have to disappear for the duration. She can tell them he's on safari in Africa, or with *Medecins San Frontieres* or something. Leave her alone. Let her be happy. She's nice. Mammy and Daddy would be proud…

"Fonsie, plaster!"

"Fuck ye!"

We'll get them bastards out of Ireland once and for all. It'll be worth it. God, I wouldn't mind a wee farm of my own, with pigs and Alpacas. Lovely.

He adjusted his cap and went down to mix plaster.

On the morning following the meeting in Cookstown, Billy McKay MP rose in the parliament in London to make a statement:

"Mr Speaker, I have it on good authority that a very prominent businessman from the Republic of Ireland has provided the money to purchase a farm near Cookstown, County Tyrone. Immediately following this purchase, the land was then transferred to the ownership of a group called The O'Neill Collective and registered on the island of Barbados in the Caribbean.

"Mr. Speaker, it is well known that this so-called O'Neill Collective is a front organisation for the IRA and nationalist agitators in Ulster and their ultimate aim is to clear loyal farmers and businesspeople from their land and possessions. What steps is the government going to take urgently to protect British citizens from the spectre of creeping ethnic cleansing in Northern Ireland?"

At the last remark, parliamentarians who had hitherto been half-asleep in the chamber during questions to the Minister for Agriculture jolted fully awake to jeer at the Member for South Belfast "Rubbish! Nonsense!"

McKay gave the speaker a cross look and sat down, pleased that his remarks had been aired and he could now go right to the top, to the P.M, where he could expect a sympathetic hearing.

Prime Minister Gerald Ashton was preoccupied. He was happy enough to participate in the collective effort to manage the Anthrax crisis in Oxfordshire, and in this regard he retained the goodwill of the populace. However, the people were anxious. House and farm prices had crashed to worthless for a ten mile radius of Chipping Norton; farms and businesses had lost everything except their savings; mortgage companies were sending out final demands, threatening foreclosure. The government would have to cover the cost.

A vast logistical operation encompassing military and civilian resources, anyone with capability and expertise, had descended on this, one of the most affluent areas of the Home Counties; not a strategic target, in military terms, but one well-chosen to strike at the beating heart of the country.

Local residents here were not the annoying flotsam and jetsam of impoverished immigrants jammed into London. These were the backstop of England. The Prime Minister's country residence was just forty miles down the motorway.

All moveable vehicles and equipment on the periphery of the Hot Zone were being driven or transported *into* the quarantine area where they could be dealt with more easily and forgotten.

Ashton knew he was under pressure. The people needed relief from the pervasive air of panic and hopelessness. In the past, he had always managed to pull a rabbit out of the hat. So sitting in his office at Number Ten watching the Agriculture debate which would normally be a bore to him, his interest was piqued by the contribution of the Belfast MP.

Northern Ireland Unionists were generally held to be troublesome Neanderthals, but in the final analysis they were Brits, holding on grimly to their remnant of Empire. On top of that, under the surface atmosphere of horror at Oxford's plight, there was a simmering impetus for revenge. And reports that the missing Anthrax pilot had turned up at a political rally in Dublin had caused a heated spat with the Republic's government.

The PM's diary showed he had a request for a meeting with McKay. This could be worth exploring…

O'Toole sat thinking, fiddling with a swatch of paper page markers. What he noticed most was the complete freedom of attitude displayed online by the young Irish with patently Catholic names as they joked, laughed, swore and pontificated on everything from soup to nuts, including the sacred cows of religion, marriage, sex, nationality and politics; an openness unknown in his young day when, in the era of Civil Rights and sectarian murder, it was necessary to have regard for the gerrymandered state you lived in and for the sensibilities of your neighbours who were at one and the same time loyal to Britain and also engaged in an insidious domination of their native Irish neighbours.

The zeitgeist declared that the people of the 1960s '70s '80s and '90s, had paid the price of this freedom, Unionism had been found out and had lost the initiative. Online was a free country. Social media makes everyone a publisher, and potential opinion leader. A united Ireland was here in all but name.

O'Toole knew it wasn't as simple as that. On the ground, those who would seek to maintain their part of Empire in this part of Ireland, were fighting a voluble, hopeful rearguard action in the face of an avalanche of native cultural and political expression that would inevitably overwhelm and swamp them in their atavistic backwater.

DD and her fellow conspirators were simply planning to hasten the demise of, and deliver the *coup de grace* to, the wounded remains of British overlordship in Ireland.

The Unionists are being invited to get out. Sign on, or get out. There will be no more cajoling, no 'let's explore your sense of Britishness'. Thin gruel, if you're a Unionist.

And the South? It's gone too. The clever boys in Dail Eireann aren't going to have a thirty-two county country handed to them by default. Bunch of chancers. They had a chance to help their fellow countrymen in the North during Bloody Sunday in Derry, to exercise the first obligation of a State – protect its citizens – and what did they do? Sent ambulances. They thought that some injured freedom marchers wouldn't want to be treated in Northern hospitals. Great bloody help.

Those Unionists who are smart enough to stay can have the South for their trouble. New state, new parliament, no state religion, no history, same rugby team. Problem solved.

O'Toole was surprised at his own thoughts, but he suspected the Unionists would never give in voluntarily. No surrender!

McKay considered his forthcoming appointment with Ashton. What did he want? McKay was around long enough to know that Ashton wouldn't normally be that pleased to meet with him. He knew where Unionists stood. There weren't many on the PM's Christmas card list. So what did he want?

Certainly a distraction from the Anthrax fallout, which was having a grinding, debilitating effect on the whole population. Flights into Heathrow were being cancelled in the mistaken belief that the airport was within contagion distance of the Oxfordshire exclusion area. There would be no Ashton gung-ho solution to that, so he would be looking elsewhere to exercise his talents for mercenary war and destabilisation.

Ashton didn't like the Irish in general very much. They're a jolly lot, box above their weight in PR terms, and can turn the world green on St. Paddy's Day, but for all that they're still a bunch of clod-hoppers and chancers and an endless aggravation to England.

So when McKay arrived at Number Ten, they got down to business with the minimum of ceremony and civility. McKay outlined his case: This land deal, he asserted, was part of an exercise in ethnic cleansing of the Unionist population. To bolster his point, he produced photographs and newspaper reports of a meeting outside Drogheda two years before showing the same people now running The Movement at a "'One People, One Nation' meeting in which they deliberately defaced the Irish Tricolour flag to denote the exclusion of any Loyal Protestant participation in a new state. "And as you know, Prime Minister, Protestants were done down by the majority Papists when the Irish Free State was set up in 1922."

People loyal to The Crown would be squeezed out of mid-Ulster, he said, and forced to retreat up the M1 corridor towards Belfast. Into a ghetto! And it's only a short step from there to our complete exclusion from the island; our home!

This outfit called The Movement is nothing but a front for radical nationalists and their Concordat or '*Affirmation*' as they call it is nothing but a mailing list of those who do, and don't, support an overthrow of the existing order.

McKay and his cronies might be dismissed as a bunch of misfits and alarmists, but Ashton was aware that McKay knew his stuff and was one of the best informed politicians in Ireland. "What do you want me to do?"

"We have to preserve the democratic process and the Assembly in Northern Ireland. I know we'll be outvoted by Catholics in a few years, but not all of them want a United Ireland. And without pressure being applied by Dublin, the Assembly at Stormont will continue to exist. There would be no move to do away with it. The Republic of Ireland has no appetite to absorb a million unionists into their electoral system. They have it too good down there. So *we* are still your best gateway to Ireland.

"We have to expose and stop this 'Movement' and show it for what it is; *the happy face of the IRA.*" McKay glowered.

The meeting had gone exactly as Ashton had anticipated. He thanked McKay for his visit and promised to be in touch.

The big one was Belfast. There was going to be three assembly points; Casement Park in the south, Belfast Castle in the north and Stormont Castle in the East. All would converge on Belfast City Hall. Parades going through both nationalist and unionist areas should aim to allay any suspicion of sectarian division in The Movement. Police and The Parades Commission had been informed of the routes and were fully involved in ongoing oversight.

Nothing less than a change of state was being advocated; no Northern or Southern bias, no religious bias, no political party bias. Unionists and nationalists would be equally invited to configure the State – after it had been formed. Only one commitment was required – sign an affirmation of loyalty to Ireland.

The Movement was generally welcomed in nationalist areas in Northern Ireland, with interesting pockets of dissent from Sinn Fein who could see a loss of power and influence. With the Good Friday Agreement and the effective conclusion of the military struggle between the Irish and the British, Sinn Fein had been building a strong constitutional constituency, but were resented by many conservative nationalists for their left-wing, liberal, social policies.

The reaction in unionist areas was also interesting. Whereas there might have been expected total opposition to any initiative which did not involve continuation of the union with Britain, there was not total condemnation of the initiative on the media Talk shows. This was because of a fundamental truism of Unionism: it is not irrevocably against a united Ireland, depending on the condition of that Ireland.

Certainly there was no prospect of unity when the Irish Republic was an impoverished, Catholic-dominated basket case with an anti-British constitution. But now that was all gone, changed utterly. Indeed, many conservative Protestants could now make common cause with conservative Catholics who despaired at the so-called modernisation of society over abortion, same-sex marriage and other perversions. To many, these moral strictures were a more important signifier than some hazy union with a British establishment which wished they would go away.

Unionists noted that The Movement had not taken, and would not take, a position on these matters, and if its existence served to clip the wings of the despised Sinn Fein, it might be worth consideration.

On top of all that, most clear-eyed unionists knew the game was up. Their demise was only a question of When and How. If this 'Movement' took off without them, there could be a return to civil strife, and who could the out-voted unionists look to then..?

Gerald Ashton was beginning to see an opportunity - to do what he did best. A general election was due in eight months, and the parliamentary arithmetic showed he needed to keep the Northern Ireland unionists onside. The country was in a catatonic state; Contagion? The babies? More attacks? To do nothing would be lethal.

The Sunday of the Belfast parades dawned bright and cheerful. Cappuccino bars opened early for the expected influx and were rewarded with a plethora of media and journalists. Bus loads of stewards, their yellow jackets now embossed with the distinctive image of the Raven, were gathering to be further dispersed along the routes.

PSNI (Police Service of Northern Ireland) mini-buses were crammed into side streets. Back in the bad old days, the sole function of their predecessors, the Royal Ulster Constabulary, would have been to isolate Catholic/Nationalist marchers and beat the hell out of them. Nowadays the PSNI has more Catholic officers (and whistleblowers) and an unsympathetic world media scrutinising their every move. Still, they were aware of their baggage, so a low profile was to be kept – By order!

The emphasis of the day's activities was to be on celebrating Ireland in its music, sport and culture At twelve noon, an interesting development; from the three departure areas departed three horse-drawn floats, each driven by a jarvey and decked out in bunting and arrays of Movement flags. The floats were accompanied by young men and women giving hand-outs to shoppers, by-standers and church goers. 'Rejoice in Ireland, *your country*. Team up with The Movement. Sign the Affirmation. Make a safe, worthwhile future for yourself and your family.' Collection boxes rattled. In return for your donation, however small, you received a sticky badge of the raven flag with 'Your Ireland' in raised print below.

Some snarled "stuff it"; tourists were delighted. The floats clip-clopped down Falls Road, Antrim Road and Ormeau Road, speakers playing pleasant, Sunday morning songs the people would know. The collectors reported back on their phones; "reaction ok or neutral".

The day being fine, an enormous marquee had been set up in front of Belfast City Hall, with a trail of electric wires to a giant outside broadcast lorry. The marquee was manned by a group of techy-types who busied themselves checking four rows of computer screens which were set up with databases from the Voters List. Registration would cease at six o'clock to allow people to get back to their transport in daylight.

It had been a battle in City Council to get permission for this set-up. It was being sold as 'Your City, Your Country, Your Land'. Some councillors condemned it as an IRA plot; others welcomed it, "We, The People, have enough confidence to express ourselves and know what is ours. What about you?"

Upon arrival at City Hall, marchers would be funnelled down these rows of computers where they would identify themselves on the Voters List and check a tick-box to signify their commitment to the Affirmation and a second box to confirm they had not already signed. Honour system. The text of the Affirmation was available everywhere. It was not complicated or flowery in its language. A simple vow, a child could state it with ease:

AFFIRMATION
(date)

'I hereby pledge and affirm my allegiance to Ireland undivided'.

'I declare that I have not already signed this Affirmation'.

First, Establish the Nation -
then make of it what you will.

Chapter 5

Henry Ponsonby was a strong farmer with nearly six hundred acres of good land resting comfortably under the Mourne mountains near Banbridge in County Down. He had a fine herd of one hundred and seventy Holstein Friesian milking cows and two hundred Aberdeen Angus beef cattle, and his two giant, blue feed hoppers in the concreted farm yard were a landmark in these parts of which he was quietly proud. He was a well-respected man.

This was solid, settled Protestant heartland and Henry was seen to observe the proprieties of his religion and heritage and, being the man he was, no one questioned the depth of his sincerity when he dutifully marched with the Orangemen or distained unnecessary work on the Sabbath.

Although a fit man himself, aside from a niggle in a leg, he was glad of the help of his three sons Edwin, Tom and Iain. They were sound, able men, and their work on the farm meant that outside help could be kept to a minimum. With the aid of various European grants, the farm was well equipped with machinery including a telehandler ('great machine altogether'), two 7000 series heavy tractors and sundry other tractors, bailers, trailers, harrows and muck spreaders.

There was a twin-bay drive-in automated milking parlour and details of the milk yield per cow, AI dates, records of scour, medicines and calving, were readily available on the computerised information system in the pump room.

The oldest son Edwin had always had an interest in machinery and had a collection of vintage Massey Ferguson tractors which allowed him to trade in spare parts with other enthusiasts and the general public. His best time of day was when the work was done and friends came round to talk piston compression or spray tinwork or strip an engine.

Young Iain was courting a girl from Tandragee, so he was likely to be at the cinema or at the banger racing near Rathfriland.

Tom, the middle brother, was a reserve policeman. In the olden days, he might have been in the RUC or the UDR (Ulster Defence Regiment), organisations dedicated to preserving the link with

England. That would have made him a marked man. Nowadays a reserve policeman was seen more as a preserver of the peace.

Their mother Judith kept them fed and watered and respectably dressed before they stepped out. By any measure, a model family, God-fearing, salt of the earth.

The entrance to the farm – 'Mourne Meadows' – was a well-surfaced grey, concrete road, with a pleasing dog-leg bend half way up. Lining the road side was a swathe of very happy sunflowers over six feet high, their open faces following the regular traffic proceeding towards the red brick main house.

Near the main gate was a mound of straw bales topped-off by a pair of spectacles fashioned from old tractor tires and a smiley iris of sunflower in the centre of either tire. All was stability, serenity and comfort.

So when the neighbours trickled in on Sunday morning to survey the devastation, view the remains of the barns, the warped metal, the stinking rubber and animal flesh, there lay a leaden, crushing silence. Black-faced firemen tidied up as best they could. Edwin, Iain and Tom, still in his PSNI Reservist uniform, fumbled aimlessly through the rubble. Henry stood alone by his grain hoppers, his expression distant and confused, supporting himself with a walking stick. There was no talk of politics, no retribution, no recrimination, only the overpowering understanding that this was about land; and land is lineage, land is family, land is the soul of the man, land is everything.

The Prime Minister's Parliamentary Private Secretary was feeling harried. He didn't want to waken the PM this early, but McKay was raging mad and using intemperate language on the phone – since 6.30 am. The PPS could see the news reports as well as anyone else. The farm, and now this march in Belfast; Incendiary! He had to waken the PM.

"Prime Minister, I told you, and now look what's happened," roared McKay. "This is a concerted push by extreme nationalists in Northern Ireland. I've spoken to people in Dublin; even they are on high alert. How can we hold back loyalist reaction now? Tell me that!"

Ashton was taken aback for he hadn't thought events would come to a head this quickly. You can't blame people for buying land, even if it is held by some shelf company in Barbados. But arson is different. He consoled McKay. He'd have the Northern Ireland Secretary make a statement. And he'd get some more people into The Movement to add to existing resources.

But he warned McKay; "We can't afford to have any unrest at this march today. It is perfectly legitimate. Any reaction by loyalists will have the world media down around our ears. Your P.R. is poor enough without a return to the seventies."

"People are nervous. They're your people. They expect protection. They're *entitled* to protection," answered McKay.

Ashton was seized by caution. He couldn't overreact. His calculation over the Thor catamaran incident on the Thames had been flawed; an embarrassment. He couldn't afford another screw up. But he couldn't leave Northern Ireland Unionists in the lurch. He had to intervene, if only to keep the loyalists off the streets.

Crawford Gainsworthy was well positioned. As Social & Media correspondent with The Belfast Sentinel for the past twelve years, he went to all the best do's, was welcome at society weddings and sports events, and covered the crowd at the pubs round the university for the weekend photo edition. The bright young things bought it to see pictures of themselves.

He liked The Sentinel; he had the run of the place. He liked the name; strong, silent, alert. He was content that the Union appendix of Northern Ireland, although increasingly remote from the Mainland, continued to revolve on its axis as nature and conquest intended it to do, for the time being.

But he had noticed the change. Since the peace agreement, the unionist hegemony was losing ground. Catholics, especially the young, were taking to social media with their thoughts on everything from music to politics, and without a by-your-leave from anyone. They were winning the PR battle by a long way. The enemy was at the gates. This must be how they felt in the last days of the Raj; isolated, unloved, fading.

Howandever; stories to be written, pics to be taken, champagne to be swallowed. A Catholic friend – yes, he did have catholic friends – was meeting him at Casement Park GAA stadium to arrange a photo shoot for the stadium's upcoming 75th anniversary.

Not many years ago, The Sentinel would not have covered the anniversary – it would have been considered a catholic/nationalist conspiracy, probably attended by IRA elements who were held inseparable from GAA supporters. Coverage would have given comfort to the enemy.

Now it would be given prominence in the GAA page of the sports section, just as the nationalist papers covered protestant/British sports such as hockey, soccer and rugby.

Driving up the Falls Road towards the stadium at Andersonstown brought to him the fragility of his family's situation. It was common knowledge that some protestant families had fled the outer reaches of provincial Ulster and were moving towards Belfast for security. It wouldn't be that desperate for people who had transportable skills and businesses, but for his family who were farming near Cookstown, it was becoming a problem. Their neighbouring catholic farmers were civil enough with a "Howrya Willie, middling prices" at the cattle mart, but they knew these same farmers would be forced to take sides when the time came.

Kevin McRory was waiting for him. Kevin was secretary of his GAA club, the Falls Fianna, and Gaelic Games correspondent for the Belfast Sentinel and Radio North. Meeting regularly in the course of their professional work, they shared a sense of humour and, if mention of local religious difficulties were kept to a minimum, they got along well, disparaging politicians on all sides, especially the Brits.

Kevin was an engaging companion and talented footballer, confident of his ability in any company.

The anniversary was to be celebrated over the weekend of the 7th - Friday evening, céilí and folk music in the marquee, with an open mic; Saturday, a series of exhibition football, camogie and hurling games from kids to veterans from all over Ireland; Sunday, speeches at noon followed by the big game, an Ulster 15 against the rest of Ireland, throw-in 2pm. Thirty thousand spectators and supporters expected.

Following the game, many would take part in the parade to Belfast City Hall. Marching bands, floats. A celebration of all good things Irish. At City Hall, all will be invited to sign an Affirmation of their loyalty to, and faith in, Ireland, accepting the manifest rewards and responsibilities of citizenship.

Gainsworthy wasn't stupid, he could see it for what it was; an aggressive statement of Irish cultural nationalism, take it or leave it. It was a rallying cry to those who were unsure, unconcerned or ambivalent. It was time to make your mark.

It was a mirror image to the Ulster Covenant signed in September 1912 by half a million Empire Loyalist men and women who protested a proposed Home Rule bill that would attempt to reverse the Plantations that gave protestant invaders their land, their livelihood and their hegemony in Ireland.

Following its initiation in Belfast, the Affirmation computers would then accompany The Movement on a tour of all Ireland, inviting all the people to rejoice in the unparalleled promise of the Irish nation.

Gainsworthy and his friend Kevin McRory left the bar at Casement Park clubhouse and out into the morning to witness the start of the parade. Crossing the car park, Gainsworthy was surprised to see two men he knew, Wesley Knipe and Josh Stockman, both of Old Cregagh rugby club, putting their sports kit into the boot of a car. "They're Prods! What are they doing here?"

"They're learning Gaelic football."

"What, the catching and kicking and that stuff?"

"Yea. It's a skills thing the provincial rugby teams are trying to improve on. Stockman had a decent tour of Japan last month, but his defensive work wasn't great, so they want him to work on it."

"Fair enough."

They had discussed the Affirmation and were content with their decision whether to sign or not sign when the time came. They had also discussed the incidents which had gripped the news channels all morning. It was obvious to anyone with an eye to see it that the fire at the Banbridge farm was arson and the work of modern-day Whiteboys. The land would be bought or taken. A carrot and a stick; together they serve to concentrate minds.

Gainsworthy stayed close to his friend at the beginning. This was a march of The People. Today, he was not of The People, but he knew there would be no violence, no coercion. So, leaning upon his friend, he resolved to enjoy the occasion for the entertainment it offered and to document it for the history it would become. He carried his notepad and pen and camera and took photos as they presented themselves, for this was a significant social event.

People joined the parade; "Howrya Eamonn?" "Y'allright Josie?" And along the route, musicians, stewards and actors.

The reporter observed a good number of pipers and the complicated Uilleann (Elbow) pipes with their enormously stirring martial sound.

"There's a Pipers' Festival on to coincide with the parade. It's to remember a famous meeting of pipers in Belfast in 1792. Most of the pipers were Prods, you know, 'cause they were the only ones could afford a set of pipes in those days. You'll see them down at City Hall later on."

Gainsworthy felt slightly guilty. He knew the pipers were his people, but their significance had not dawned on him. He couldn't tell McRory, but he felt he was being overwhelmed by a wave of Irishness and cultural depth that was admirable but that he barely recognised or had come to terms with. He lived on the island of Ireland, but his existence here had been on the surface of the island, looking east, with no aspiration to explore its depth.

He had some Presbyterian friends who appreciated the contribution of the protestant faith to Irish music, language and statehood over the centuries, a contribution that must be kept to quiet, academic corners while a besieged community struggled for existence.

And on this day, he knew what he was being sold. For there is no more potent way of achieving political ends than by rousing ordinary people through their folk memory of poetry, plays and songs. Behind him he heard people discussing: "I think it's an awful pity of that man in Banbridge, his whole life work gone".

"It's hard. But listen, lads, his people were planters. They took advantage often enough. They were like the Boers in South Africa. They always knew their day would come."

"Are you going to sign, Fred?"

"But sure you can't be on the march and not sign!"

"Yes you can. I'm only here because I work with you bunch. My ma was very upset. She says she's scared. She said I should see what it's like and tell the family. If it's IRA, we won't sign, regardless."

"I don't think it's IRA, but it's certainly very nationalist. You know, in another country, like Canada, this would be a big national day for *everybody*. What would you do, Vinnie, if you had to sign or bugger off?"

"I'm signing anyway to force the issue, even though it's coercion. It can't go on the way it's going. Unionists have to shit or get off the po. They can't hold the island to ransom forever."

"Ever the well-worked phrase, Vinnie. If it's coercion, what's the music and sports for? Who's forcing you?"

"As my good friend Mr. Billy McKay M.P. says, the music and dancing is a papish scam, to sweeten the pill."

"Your head's a marley. If you're being screwed, you might as well lie back and enjoy it."

"That's all very well for you lot. If the Whiteboys attacked us, where would we go? We have no relatives in England or Scotland. If they took our house, what the fuck would we do? We'd have to start fighting all over again."

"What's wrong with signing and staying in Ireland?"

"This is *Northern* Ireland."

"It's dead. It doesn't exist, mate. Save yourself."

"You can't have a United Ireland if you don't have a united people. And you haven't got that. Fuck!"

Crawford Gainsworthy got tense and began to think he had done the wrong thing. Where would *he* go? He wished he was home in Newtownabbey. Beside him, Kevin McRory had also heard the exchanges. "Nothing will happen today, unless there's a loyalist attack. Will there be an attack?"

"How the hell would I know? I'm not privy to that stuff."

"The way I look at it is, it's your country – if you want it. So enjoy it. There'll be great music at City Hall, you'll get good copy for tomorrow, and we'll go back to Casement after for a pint and the dancing…"

It wasn't hard to see what was going to happen. Once the Secretary of State made her statement to the news channels at 10 a.m., having pointedly gone to the steps of Government Buildings at Stormont to decry the incident at the farm and uphold the right to peaceful assembly, the organisers of The Movement knew the ball was in play. Stewards were told again – with emphasis – Keep to the plan; no deviation; stamp out any trouble immediately.

The new flag, the floats, the actors, the Affirmation, the pipers' festival, the absence of any parliamentary or political personalities in the vanguard of the parade; All served to give no identifiable target for protestors or agitators.

O'Toole stayed near the back. He was conscious of events racing ahead of him. They had never been within his control anyway. He was beholden for his job and his flat. He was in thrall to a letter he had never opened. He was receiving notes and updates from DD. She was an architect of events and a planner of agendas; he was a pawn, preoccupied with how to keep his dignity.

His life was not unpleasant. He enjoyed his work – was grateful for it – and was conducting an undemanding relationship with Maire, a relationship which fulfilled his minimal quota of personal interaction.

On Tuesday evening they had voyaged down to Sligo to watch the Connacht junior showjumping team score a splendid victory in the Western European league. Thence to the fine French restaurant at Mullaghmore for supper and convivial chat. Maire was charming and fun as always, apparently content with his company, as he with her's. He was grateful for her avoiding discussion on his recent history and relationships, though he was quite sure she was aware, in detail. She was not the kind of woman to leave things to chance.

At this stage, his health was fairly good. The back pain which had plagued him for years had gone away. He put that down to the course of acupuncture and the horse riding; 'the best medicine for the inside of a man is the outside of a horse'. So a natural inclination to fuss and take care of him was not her motivation. He was content they were good friends, and they were both 'of an age'. To keep up, he made sure he did some reading on the music in her forthcoming recitals if only to be able to contribute sensibly to any discussion which might arise.

As to horses, she knew as much as he and they both retained a wide-eyed enjoyment and admiration for these the most noble of God's creatures.

Near the junction of Grosvenor Road and Falls Road, the parade was joined by a troupe of mummers and wrenboys with the head of an ass, a cock, a devil, sheaves of straw from head to foot, wickermen. They danced and cavorted in front of the parade and gave out their sticky brooches to by-standers in return for a reasonable donation. Miserable contributions were rewarded by a whack to the head from a papier-mache cudgel, and they danced on.

Next, two fit-looking youths, clothed in beaten copper mail and laced sandals and spears, came forth with great shouts and admonishments to enact the battle of Ferdia and Cú Chullain at the ford of Ulster. Druidic personages in oakleaf garlands gave out leaflets of explanation – the players were actors and extras from the movie on the life and deeds of the hero Cú Chullain currently being shot on locations all over Ireland.

They set upon each other, egged on by the warrior woman Scathach in her bloodied robes and dirt-stained face. The parade halted. Gainsworthy came forward boldly to take photographs from every angle, his apprehension somewhat alleviated by the opportunity for honest toil.

The battle raged, the players grunted, cried and thrusted, the warrior woman screeched. Cú Chullain, greatest of the heroes, danced and mimed the red rage of battle, the *riastradh*. Then, the inevitable; he gripped and cast *Gae Bolga*, the spear of mortal pain, and Ferdia was no more. A great sorrow descended. Then the people cheered and clapped, the players bowed, and the parade moved on.

O'Toole, who had circumvented the crowd to witness the battle, was touched by admiration and pride as he considered the myths and stories we give ourselves and which add greatly to our sense of identity and self-esteem. He set off brightly in the sunshine.

On an advertising hoarding, the appellation 'Belfast Child' over an image of George Best.

Further on, a hoarding with a likeness of the blind harper Turlough O'Carolan under the title 'Renaissance Man'.

And yet again, a montage: Countess Markievicz, Gráinne Mhaol O'Malley, Maureen O'Hara, Jocelyn Bell Burnell, Anne Devlin, Lady Augusta Gregory, Bernadette Devlin, Maria Edgeworth; 'Women of Ireland'.

And 50 yards further, a giant composite "Gentlemen of High Renown". It was fortunate the faces had names, for he would not have recognised some. But certainly there was Brendan Behan, Nicky Racard, the Pride of Wexford, together Vincent O'Brien and John Magnier, a likeness of Henry Joy McCracken, proud Ulster Presbyterian, the tenor John McCormack, Willie John McBride, an 1844 calotype of the radical songsmith Thomas Moore and close by, an image of the bard from Clare, Brian Merriman along with his most eloquent translator Frank O'Connor. And amid these human gentlemen, the great equine hero Arkle. He recognised the 'slightly constitutional' Sean Lemass and the commanding Michael Collins, but had to look closely to identify the American patriarch Thomas Mellon, once a farmer's boy from Tyrone. Daniel O'Connell, the King of the Gypsies was accompanied by Monsignor Hugh O'Flaherty, the Scarlet Pimpernel of the Vatican. It was time to move on.

Where Falls Road meets Divis Street, the parade was joined by a motley lot of hurlers, camogie, soccer and rugby players in their strips, throwing the balls around or just walking with the marchers. The good weather was a blessing on the day. Gainsworthy had no shortage of material for his notebook and camera. He tried to keep the underlying motives in focus and not be seduced by the jazz and glitz. He could assume that the hurlers and camogie players were from the nationalist camp, and he was most anxious to have a word with the rugby players whom he suspected might also be nationalists despite rugby's general association with the Protestant/Planter tradition. So he got in lockstep with one of the rugby players, and avoiding invasive questions, found out he was on the Academy panel at Ulster, 'but if the reporter wanted to know more, he should speak to big Geordie Wilson who, as far as he knew, was speaking later at City Hall'.

The reporter was shocked. Geordie Wilson was a famous rugby player, had played at Lock for Ireland and had been a stalwart of Ulster rugby for the past six years. Geordie was 'saved', a church-going man who had already expressed views on personal morality. On the rugby field, the management and players were concerned about his ability to win lineout ball, not which church he went to. In fact, he was held in some regard for his religious convictions.

"Where is he?" asked Gainsworthy.

"He's at City Hall, and he has some people with him. You might be surprised."

Wilson was pleased to wear the green jersey of Ireland, a uniform that would see him welcomed and honoured in any gathering, social, cultural or sporting, anywhere in the world. A seminal influence in their lives, success on the field of play was expressed in different ways. Often the players retreated to a benign retirement in their protestant community, kept the party line, honoured and unmolested as men who had done enough. Some traded on their achievements and used the contacts gained to give them a leg up in life, And some were troubled, unable to reconcile their communities' embattled vision with their experience for those crucial years as a critical cog in the Irish international rugby machine.

Geordie Wilson was troubled. It wasn't that Brand Ireland was going to be the solution to everything in his life. He knew the material rewards and the applause and the recognition and thanked God for his strength of arm and speed of limb, but he had something to say that could not remain unsaid. He was young enough to have avoided 'The Troubles', but his parents had gone through them and he could only lament the uselessness of it.

He had seen the videos online of the Queen of England at the Garden of Remembrance in Dublin place a wreath and bow her head to the fighters who had defied her armies for centuries. So that was that. It was all even now. There was no point in going back; there was no point in standing still! Time to change.

He couldn't excuse the inertia and stultification of his own people; neither could he in good conscience vote for any manifestation of the IRA. There had to be a third way…

The information screens in doctors' surgeries – those which remained open – projected a bold headline in red '*Due to the present emergency, pregnant women resident anywhere within a triangle from Oxford to Banbury to Cheltenham should report directly to their nearest clearing hospital*'. People read the notice and turned away. Some fled the surgery. They knew what a 'clearing hospital' was; it was a death sentence for the foetus. The women would be subjected to triage, aborted, separated from their husbands and lovers, and sentenced to a quarantine camp where many would lose their grip on reality.

Prime Minister Ashton, his mind in a state of controlled turmoil, sat in a room in Downing Street behind a door that required thumb-print and iris-recognition access. Hand-picked operatives, under his personal supervision, manned a bank of phones and video screens. Images of marchers for facial recognition processing poured in. Phone messages from revellers and onlookers crouched in shop doorways and alleyways and from behind mummers' masks, delivered commentary on any noteworthy detail. *Strictly* no communication was made with local constabulary. Headshots of ringleaders with their case-histories, relationships and known or suspected political sympathies were catalogued and matched to Scotland Yard databases. Records of their employment, travel, bank accounts and tax returns were called up for scrutiny and comparison.

By 11 a.m., not one record had been found of any identifiable personality with a plausible case for sedition or criminal association. Nothing they didn't already know. There was nothing to pin on Robert McAdam, except his being a Protestant nationalist. Doreen Downey had been photographed in the company of paramilitaries in pubs, but then so had Margaret Thatcher. John Madden, the transport entrepreneur, was a prominent member of the Chamber of Commerce, and Irene Moloney was a noted professional golfer and broadcaster. What linked these four was that none was a member of an existing political party. The rest were strawmen and volunteers.

Turlough O'Toole was there; his flat in Bundoran had been combed. Dozens of stewards from the old Civil Rights days, hundreds of fresh-faced youths, consumed with a sense of freedom and indignant at any barrier to the march of the nation, a smattering of old internees who had long paid their dues. But no politicians, at least not in prominent positions, in the parades. The word was that no representatives of existing Irish political parties would be welcome, unless content to walk as ordinary citizens in the body of the parades.

That pilot! Where the hell is she? The anthrax was from Russia. Chances are she was too; part of the package. She'll be long gone. The Ruskies aren't going to hand her over.

On the Casement parade, Sinn Fein were noticeably absent. Their leadership feared The Movement might steal their thunder so were wary of supporting it, at least publicly.

The Stormont parade was the most interesting. Everyone acknowledged the rhetoric surrounding a United Ireland was in play, a live topic. Changed times. Many unionists condemned The Movement as progress, many hedged their bets, some joined in the festivities. There were plainly pockets of Protestants who, while not committed to the possible changes espoused by The Movement, were concerned to be on hand to influence events. And they did feel able to subscribe in an oblique way to the mantra 'Ireland Is Ours'.

So with the parade ambling through true-blue unionist areas on the Newtownards Road, the loyalist underground was holding fire, unwilling as yet to publicly associate the marchers with the Whiteboys of Banbridge.

Passing over the Albert Bridge, a group of five in the middle of the parade was picked out by the TV coverage – English and Scottish MPs! Well, that was to be expected; there was no real cohesion in British party politics anymore, and the Whips were ineffectual. Who knows how many clandestine fifth columns there were in Westminster now?

It was reported that a group of elders of the fundamentalist Free Presbyterian Church, while disapproving of this excessive gaiety on the Sabbath, were anxious to give out pamphlets on the periphery of the parade exalting The Way of The Lord.

Ashton was also holding fire. There would be no repeat of the Thor fiasco on the Thames. This group might be clean, debate on uniting Ireland was current, and there was no law against pressing your case. But there were laws against coercion and Whiteboy terror, and Ashton was confident the roots of that terror were in this group. They were acting hand-in-glove, carrot-and-stick. He knew their leaders, their financiers and their associates. McKay was right; they were trying to uproot the unionists by hook or by crook.

He wasn't concerned about the fate of Northern Ireland; it was nothing but trouble. Besides, the whole issue was irrelevant in view of what was happening in Europe. But he was concerned about the bastards who had attacked the mainland.

Chapter 6

If it could be recognised as Fonsie Sweeney, it was lying in the back of the van on the tin floor along with the tools. At first glance, it was a man with no hair and his face and torso scalded red. He had tried to throw the petrol can onto the fire but the bulbous ring on his finger had caught in the handle grip of the can as he was about to let go and the can had twisted in his hand with the petrol still flowing out. He saw the flame charging up the arc of petrol but had not time; with a percussive *bhaaatz* the can exploded. Fonsie's torso was immolated as his two companions looked on… "Fuck!"

They tried to carry him; he couldn't bear it. They found water in a tin can under the spouting and dribbled it on his arm; the flesh erupted and seeped something pale. They grabbed a sheet of corrugated tin, threw their jackets and hay netting onto it and wrapped him up as far as they could, then they stumbled and grunted down the field, past the nodding sunflowers and the fat man made of tyres and into the wood by the duck pond where they had hidden the van. The beginnings of an early dawn were slipping over the crest of the Mournes when they rocked and skidded their way out of the wood on to the road.

"Where'll we go?"

"Fuck, we can't go to the hospital. They'll ask."

"What do you put on burns?"

"I don't know. Ointment."

"Where'll we take him?"

"Maureen's."

"We can't take him there; her husband's a Gard."

"Jesus. We could call Mickey Lennon."

"Sure he's not a doctor."

"Isn't he at university?!"

"He's studying biology, for fuck's sake!"

In the back of the van, Fonsie heard the frantic conversation as a blur. His eyes were sealed shut, his eyelids welded together. Where his arms touched the undulating hay netting, he could feel only that they were swimming. He knew that was the skin coming off and his arms oozing. Everything was yellow searing pain. His only relief was to feel his heels in his shoes, the sense of what it used to be. He was falling, falling. He had no desire for control. His mind did not work, beyond bearing the pain. If he could only accept the yellow scorching, then ordinary pain felt better. His palms were face-down on the corrugated tin. If he could clear his mind enough, he would try to touch the tin with a finger; his fingers did not recognise the signal. He could not tell if his fingers moved at all. He could feel nothing that told him any part of his body had made a new contact with his tin shroud. If he let go, he was confident he would quietly die. They said he started screaming "Aaaagh! Aaaagh! Aaaagh!", over and over. His two companions were gripped by an even greater panic; if they had to stop at a junction or a traffic light, his cries in the early Sunday morning air would be heard. People would stare, take their number.

"Call DD!"

"Why?"

"She might know. She's a bloody scientist."

"There's no point..." They found themselves shouting above his cries. Their shouts, his cries, intermingled and reverberated off the tin sides of the van. The driver began to lose his judgement. He swiped the kerb. He wound down his window to let the noise out. Fresh air buffeted his eyes; he wound the window up again. His companion called "Go to Keady, go to Keady." Keady meant the barn. If they could get to the barn, they could get him out of the van; let him scream to the sheep, to the fields. Clear the foul cries from the van. They could walk; run! Their feet were lashed by chains to their heads in terror, their eyes knotted to their fingers. "Aaaagh! Aaaagh! Aaaagh!" Their fingers were locked at the joints; he couldn't steer the van; his leg pressed the brake instead of the clutch; the van lurched; the body rolled. "Aaaagh! Aaaagh!" His calls cleaved the air.

It is twenty-four miles from Banbridge to Keady. If you know your way, you can avoid towns, early morning villages and crossroads, except Tandragee. You have to go up the hill in Tandragee. "There won't be anybody awake in Tandragee. It's

Prod." Coming to the 30mph sign outside Tandragee, the driver tried to flex his locked fingers, tried to get a grip. He couldn't look back at the source of the screams. He wound his window tight and turned on the radio; the Farming programme. He tried to press a button, but hit two. Static. He pressed with his thumb; Irish airs. He turned up the volume. To the swell of The Londonderry Air, they drove up Tandragee hill. Maybe Fonsie would faint. But his screams mingled with the music and the rattle of terror in their heads. Not a soul. Out into the country, towards Clare.

Patsy McGlone's barn was open on three sides, for bales. In the old days, the Brits would land a helicopter, search the barn for arms, and buzz off. It wasn't a dump. It was always kept clean for emergencies, so they would leave it alone. Fonsie parked the cattle truck there. Everybody knew whose it was, so nobody touched it.

When they reached the rutted lane to the barn, they could slow down. The driver shouted "Fonsie, Fonsie, we're in Keady. You'll be ok." Whether he heard or not, they didn't know. They pulled in beside the lorry. "Put bales in the lorry!" They let down the lorry ramp and, knowing they could do nothing else, they ran with the bales, released from their chains. They each had tears in their eyes, for there was no reason to be coy. They called to Fonsie as they ran; "We're making a bed for you, Fonsie. It'll be nice." They pulled the binder twine from the bales and scattered the hay amid the sweet smell of manure. They pulled the sheet of tin from the van and walked it folded like a half moon up the ramp. "Fonsie! Fonsie! We're going to lift you."

Fonsie was a hard man. A raparee most of his life, a man who lived on the edge and made no plans. A man who stayed loose. A man who would put his hand in the flame. A cruel man who could take the knocks. A slight man but vicious. A man who despised your weaknesses and your veneer.

Now he had to face the fire, again. How would they lift him? He would crumble. His torso was weeping; his back would be the same. Pieces of his shirt were stuck to his body. He had to come off the tin; what would he leave behind? They couldn't lift his arms and feet; his arms were boiled red. His boots were on his feet. They would have to lift him from the side so he wouldn't drag on the tin. They sat the tin on a bale and wriggled their arms under his backside. His trousers were intact. Where their hands met underneath his body, they intertwined their fingers and, with great love for a man, they lifted and grunted. There was no sound. The lifters looked at each other, questions in their eyes. "Go on. Go on!" They pressed into him, hoping he had not died. It was too late to stop. The tears in their eyes overflowed as they edged him to the bed of hay and laid him down. There was no sound. He was in shock, or dead. "Call Johnsie."

They knew enough not to lay anything on top of him, but fanned him with doubled-up plastic bags. He breathed; they breathed.

Forty minutes later, an ambulance rocked up the lane in the mist grey, and Fonsie's brother Johnsie got out. They showed him where Fonsie lay. "Why didn't you take him to Daisy Hill hospital, for fuck's sake?"

They whispered to him, for the two ambulance attendants were ministering to the prone body with cotton and morphine, "They'd ask us how it happened."

"That doesn't matter! Look at him, he's going to die. Fuck!"

They sheathed him in silver wrapping and transported him to the ambulance. The attendants were mute and embarrassed, for they still had their lives to live. There was little mystery to this. With Johnsie in the back, muttering emollients to his brother who answered with his eyes, the ambulance took off with all decent speed towards Newry. Clarity now descended; the two firebombers sped off towards the Irish Republic.

With a giant sculpture of the Brown Bull of Cooley to the fore, followed by the warring queens of Connacht and Ulster, the Antrim Road parade proceeded in good-natured disarray towards Belfast city centre.

Passing Hopefield Avenue, stewards unobtrusively lined the right-hand side of the road to distract from the Black Marias which were lined up down the centre of the avenue. The chief steward gave a desultory wave to the officers and passed on. Facial recognition cameras picked out two well known faces in tandem; prominent talk-show host Damien Devenney and Ingrid Toal, award-winning children's writer, lately the recipient of an OBE in the King's Honours List for her services to literature.

A regular on Northern Ireland media, she was a lively contributor, noted for her uncompromising opinions on the quality of young teachers in the education system, half of whom, she held, were unable to speak the language properly and were in dire need of elocution lessons. So how could they possibly educate children when they can't speak the language properly, and *enunciate*?

Her outspoken views were certainly influential in the current debate regarding the bi-annual assessment of Secondary teachers at the Teachers' Union conferences.

Her opinions on national politics were less well known, but few would have contested her right to join battle on any of these questions. Damien Devenney had always found her 'great value', so was pleased to be seen in her company. And she in his.

She especially objected to people, particularly young women, speaking in an assumed American drawl with an irritating tick in the back of their throat, as if their batteries were running down. She caused quite a stir when she reprimanded a BBC reporter, live on air, for this very irritating deficiency.

Her reason for being on the parade, she said, was the obvious and manifest trouble the border caused, and she could see no reason why Unionists, given sufficient gumption, could not influence and engineer a 32-county Irish state into a benign and mutually-beneficial relationship with Britain and Europe. She was going to sign the Affirmation.

Which was an interesting counterpoint to two, well-dressed men walking a short distance behind. Joe Donnelly and Packie Skevington worked together at a big solicitors' office in Belfast. They played Gaelic football together, and both knew Kevin

McRory. They came from families with impressive nationalist credentials – and they were not going to sign.

They were engaged in banter with one of the stewards: "Why are you here, lads? Yer only taking up room."

"It's like this, Mickey; the North gets a subvention every year from Britain of nine billion quid. Nine billion! Free money! Now we are Irishmen, same as the rest. But that doesn't mean we're stupid. We are in a market of sixty million people, not five million, like Ireland. We can embarrass the Brits into giving us more at the drop of a hat, and you want us to cut ourselves off from that? That's the stupidest thing I've heard all day. You're all half mad. So we're going to walk with you down the town for the craic, then we're going to fuck off to the Titanic Centre and have a few pints."

"Yis are a disgrace. Your da would turn in his grave, Packie Skevington."

"It was this bloody lark that sent him to his grave, Mickey. He did his bit, and what did it get him?"

"He was a better bloody man than you."

"Fuck off, Mickey."

Behind locked doors, with one eye on the parades, P.M. Ashton considered the briefing papers in front of him. Top of the pile was 'The O'Neill Collective'. To some it was a fanciful notion, *'being a cooperative to receive and manage those lands and other assets returned from the unlawful possession of invaders and usurpers for the eventual use and benefit of the people of Ireland'*. Not a lot different to the Crown Estates, if you think about it.

A perusal of the Board of Advisors of this outfit made it seem less fanciful. Several names he recognised; all were accompanied by comprehensive biographical detail. There were the figureheads; a former president of Ireland, a retired Taoiseach, and twelve or more prominent business people from America, Australia, Monte Carlo, Ireland and, surprisingly, two from Britain.

Without exception, they were from the ranks of the mega-rich and powerful; chemicals, software, manufacturing, electronics, property, sport, broadcasting, music. This was the Irish diaspora in action.

He knew some had a track-record of thinly-veiled antipathy towards British activity in Ireland. Their wealth and influence left them fairly well insulated from any hostile reaction to their participation, but they would not get involved if there was an IRA presence.

Chief Executive of the organisation was one Garville Richler, a Jewish real estate operator from New York. His travel records showed he had visited Dublin three times in the past year. Banking facilities provided by First Credit Bank of New York; branches in Zurich, Dubai, London and Dublin.

Richler was undoubtedly getting his fees as a manager and would be at arm's length from the actual activities of the co-op.

But if this movement conducted its business in a professional way, they must have considerable hopes of success as these personalities wouldn't want to be associated with a flaky enterprise. They obviously had the collective wherewithal to buy up any land for sale in Northern and Southern Ireland and would restrict their activities to that. They had the potential to be the biggest and most powerful landowner in the country, taking their rents from the land to cover their costs and interest and selling on at a discounted rate to 'selected' customers nominated by the Executive board; a perfectly legitimate business. They must also be convinced that the plan will be carried through.

Belfast City Hall is an impressive lump. Built upon the Empire's success on the far oceans and the ships that fuelled it from the great Harland & Wolff shipyards of east Belfast, it echoes protestant industry and fealty; a monument to righteousness and a bastion against the feckless hordes of catholic peasantry who cowered and plotted within the shadow of its stout walls.

Faced now with the approaching throngs chanting change, the walls seemed to shrink in the spring sun and become a retreating echo of what used to be.

O'Toole was now in the middle of the crowd. He saw no value in being recognised, much less in being picked out by a television camera. All along the footpaths, interspersed by the fish and chips and burger vans, were signs proclaiming 'Your Chance to Sign The Affirmation *Today*. Follow The Crowd'. Fair enough.

The interesting sight of three Unionist councillors from Carrickfergus engaged the attention of the media. The two men and a woman explained to the microphones that they were going to sign so they could influence the reversing of the vote held in the Republic in 2018 which allowed abortion for any reason up to twelve weeks. "It seems to us that a United Ireland will come eventually", said the woman who carried a handful of leaflets, some of which she handed to her inquisitors, "and we believe that preservation of human life is a superior issue to any political border. Our kingdom is the kingdom of God. So that's why we are here today. I know that some of our colleagues do not hold this opinion, but I hope they will allow us to express our conscience on this matter. Stop this slide into depravity!"

So far, the parade was going well. No signs of trouble. O'Toole was quite enjoying the walk and his isolation in a crowd when he heard "Mr.O'Toole, isn't it?"

Adjusting to this intrusion, O'Toole was presented with an outstretched hand; "Crawford Gainsworthy; The Sentinel."

"Ah, hello?"

"It is Mr. O'Toole, isn't it?

"Yes, my name is O'Toole. Who are you?"

"Crawford Gainsworthy. I'm the Social reporter for The Sentinel. It's a Belfast newspaper."

"Yes, I know The Sentinel. But I'm afraid I wouldn't be the best candidate for your social column."

"That's alright. Do you mind if I walk with you for a wee while?"

There was no way out, and he looked a pleasant enough fellow. The ex-detective thought about his days attending football matches when it was only civil to pass the time of day with fellow supporters. "Yes, by all means."

They walked together for a minute. Nothing was said. They both looked ahead.

"I don't want to intrude on you, Mr. O'Toole. I just recognised you and I thought, as a reporter, I should at least say hello."

He would be really the first person to come up and say hello all day; everyone else studiously avoided him, so he deserved some consideration.

"That's fair enough, Mr. Gainsworthy. It's nice to have a chat, off the record, of course."

"Of course, I'm just as interested to know why you're here as, I assume, you might be about me, me being a Prod and all. And would you call me Crawford? I have a very long name and we could spend all day just getting over the formalities?"

O'Toole smiled broadly, "Crawford is grand. I'm Toby for short. So why are you here, you being a Prod, and all?"

"I was telling a catholic friend earlier, I'm only here as a reporter, for the time being anyway. This is a big event, and I've got some great pictures and interviews. Why are you marching?"

"I want it to stop. Fighting England, fighting ourselves. Those poor people in Oxford. You can't leave it to the political parties; they are too interested in self-preservation. That's why I'm here."

"I can understand that. A lot of people are worried that the North couldn't survive without Britain's support if there was a United Ireland."

"I think you may be sure that Britain would be happy to continue to support the North for some time if there was agreed unity; an age-old problem solved. The world community would rejoice, and Europe, and especially America, would have a Marshall Plan in here like lightning; and besides, the South is well-off and a combination of North and South would be a considerable economic unit. There would be changes, of course, as duplication was ironed out, but that would be solved over time."

"You're very optimistic."

"What else can you be?"

"I think Dublin doesn't want us."

"They might not have much of a choice."

"Why?"

"Because when the people vote again on the Border in a referendum, if Southerners believe there is substantial Unionist support for unity, they will vote in favour, no matter what the political parties say. I think it is The Movement's purpose to focus people on that reality."

"You're very sure."

"I'm not."

"What about my family's farm in Tyrone? Some Prods haven't got a lot, you know; a bit of land in a country we don't own, some marches every year over a three hundred year old battle between two foreign kings, some kind of religion, a poor international football team. We're foreigners under siege."

"Are you British?"

"I suppose."

"What's British?"

"Dunno. I think it's like tiramisu; I like it but I have no idea what's in it."

"Would you want to be Irish if you could?"

"Good question."

They walked on in silence, realising they had solved nothing and still had to take a chance either way.

"Tell me about The Druid."

O'Toole made no reply. He didn't hesitate or protest. He just walked, looking at his feet. Gainsworthy, a fairly tall man, scanned the heads of the parade as his request hung heavily on O'Toole's shoulders. He had never spoken voluntarily of the priest, except to DD. It was all under lock and key. And the key was nowhere to be found.

"Do you know the story?"

"I've read the reports. I'm sure you might not want to talk about it. But I have my own opinions. The planning for what he did was amazing; not that I agree with it, mind you. Those murders. But how did he get a top secret list of MI5 spies? And that ship! We were following that on the TV for days, in the office. And I can tell you, just between us, when he sailed that ship under Tower Bridge, we cheered. It was like watching cowboys and Indians, and he had become the good guy. Amazing... Is he bonkers?"

"No, he's not bonkers. He's a very clear thinker. He's very logical and, funny enough, a man of great principle. You can ask how can a man be principled and yet be complicit in some horrendous murders. That's a reasonable question, and we who live, perhaps, fairly hum-drum lives and have a half-baked opinion on everything, might not be able to reconcile his actions with his calling. But he's a driven man. He sees the end justifying the means. He's very conscious... no, he's tortured, by British history in Ireland, and nothing he can do would be sufficient to redress the balance. That's the way he sees it, right or wrong. And we are only onlookers."

"Is he a nice man? Would you go for a pint with him?

"No I wouldn't. He's not a man who indulges in pints. But I can tell you one thing about him that he told me; he told me his own life was of no consequence. I suppose you have to be like that to undertake his journey. I'll tell you who he reminded me of, Mohandas Gandhi. They even look alike." O'Toole stopped, realising he was in danger of overflowing. Time to retrench.

"Will they try to burst him out?"

"What? Out of Broadmoor? I wouldn't think so. Apparently he is, em... happy enough. He has achieved a lot."

"A lot? Good?"

"I don't know. Maybe we'll have to wait on history's verdict on that."

"Fair enough. Well, it's been great talking to you. This conversation was between us, as I said. And can I say, I think you did the reasonable thing? You were in a very difficult position. I don't know what the rest of us would have done."

"You're a good man, Crawford. I hope things work out and you stay with us."

Crawford Gainsworthy moved to the side of the road, and took some time to fiddle with his camera and arrange his thoughts.

As they got nearer to the venue, the route was narrowed by crowd-control barriers until it was wide enough for three or four walkers. The floats and players and the siege banners swerved off to the collecting area in the greenery of Donegal Square, leaving the walkers a clear route towards the big marquee.

At the entrance, subscribers were asked to take the correct queue for Derry/Londonderry & Fermanagh, Tyrone & Armagh, Antrim & Down, and Other, depending upon where your vote resided. O'Toole took 'Other'.

As he stuttered along in the queue, an odd thought came into his head; the last time he was in a position like this, it was at the end of a 10K race in the Phoenix Park many years ago when we all collapsed, puffing and blowing, filled with a great sense of elation at having stayed the course, and lining up to surrender our race numbers and accept a doggie bag of goodies as a remembrance of the day. You could only smile.

He was recognised. "I don't think I'm on the Voters List."

"Ah, a recent immigrant…?"

"In a manner of speaking."

He scanned the lists for his surname. Nothing in Donegal. Lots of O'Tooles in Galway. And then, as if by magic, Turlough O'Toole and his address in Ballsbridge, at the apartment he had rented for years. A previous life.

He asked nametag Deirdre, the student database expert, if he could sign at his previous address. "Yes, as long as you tick the undertaking that you will sign only once. Honour system."

O'Toole stood upon his honour and before he had time to think, he had signed the Affirmation. All his scruples had come to nought. He was now a fully committed Irishman.

In the days following the Belfast parade, O'Toole was brighter. He had signed the Affirmation. He had a home again, a country. He even felt like taking a view on politics.

As he lived above the shop, it was no inconvenience to be first in, sort the post and emails and get the kettle on. Daithi was always on time and content to talk, or not, as the occasion demanded, so they had half an hour to fiddle about before opening the doors at 8.30 a.m. Most shops in the middle of town opened at 9 a.m., but O'Toole thought it was a good idea to open early to attract strays and browsers, especially as his Coffee Dock was now open.

On Wednesday morning he went down with the keys. He heard his name called. Maire, parked on the other side of the street. She hurried over, distressed. "Can I come in?"

He quickly opened the door. "Captain Butchart-Grimley has been attacked. His barns burnt. Three cows are dead. The Gardai are there, and the fire engines. But there's nothing to save. His horses were out, thank God."

He had never seen her perturbed. She was a near neighbour of the Captain and they got on well. He used to joke with her concerning any possible romantic liaisons: "What's it like playing second fiddle?"

She was more sad than cross. O'Toole expressed no view but made them both tea. He wondered would it be cowardly if he, a 'fully committed Irishman', let her make the political analysis when a friend was involved. She saved him; "Toby, I wish this was all over. There's too much misery. James Butchart-Grimley is a good man, but he is committed to Britain, with his history, as you might expect."

"What will he do now?"

"I don't know. I just went over this morning when I heard the fire engines to see if I could be of any use. He's shattered. I wasn't able to say much to him. He's not the type to give up. I've taken his two horses to the yard to look after them. His cousin's coming up from Ahoghill to help."

"O'Toole poured the tea. "He has to sign the Affirmation. They all have to. It's the only way they'll let him stay. It's the only way this will end."

Senator D'Arcy was not of that view. If this crowd got purchase with their extreme doctrine of Irishness and with those bloody Whiteboys creating havoc in the countryside, the Republic would be sucked deeper into Northern Ireland politics, and maybe violence, and there was no margin in that.

He called the Taoiseach and they agreed we must make contact with the British and issue a condemnation immediately. He knew James Butchart-Grimley slightly; being from the North, the Captain was entitled to dual British and Irish citizenship even though he travelled on a British passport. The Taoiseach would call the Prime Minister and by the one o'clock news, a joint statement was issued decrying the atrocity in Donegal.

Privately it was agreed that these Whiteboys now constituted a real threat and action must be taken. Ashton had his excuse.

Chapter 7

The pleasant, unhurried village of Kilkeel sits facing the sea just south of Percy French's Mountains of Mourne. As might be expected, the smell of fish and the cries of gulls dominate the town, but not in an offensive way; they just tell you what to expect...

The fleet was out when the rustbucket steamed carefully around the harbour wall. At twenty-nine feet, she was seaworthy enough but had seen better days. Her flag was the Red Hand of Ulster, her name was 'Southern Breeze'.

Late of the fishing fleet at Douglas, Isle of Man, she had recently been sold to Kelp Enterprises of Bangor, County Down, and would be based at Kilkeel for the mackerel, cod and shellfish in the Irish Sea.

It was no surprise she would arrive at 3 p.m. when the harbour was quiet after her three hour trip from Douglas. She glided to her pre-arranged berth beside the loading ramp. The gentle May sun dimpled the water; deckhands loaded crates on to lorries for distribution and trundled from the dock to their engagements with the nation's palates.

A period of calm before the fleet returned, and a few dockers wandered off towards the canteen. A curtain-side lorry edged down the ramp. A fork-lift truck ticked over in readiness; its driver took the opportunity to catch up with the sports results in the paper.

A man stepped hastily down the dock towards the ramp and engaged the fork-lift driver in what seemed to be a short and earnest conversation. The driver climbed off the machine, leaving his newspaper, and accompanied the messenger up the ramp.

On the Southern Breeze, the crewmen readied a cargo for unloading. The gulls wheeled and squealed, the only really energetic activity in the harbour, so that when the bomb exploded with little more than a *wromph*, most paid no attention, certainly not the people in the canteen who assumed it was the normal crash and bang of daily activity.

The second *wromph* did claim attention as it was quickly followed by splashing as heavy items fell into the sea from a height.

When the body of a man stretched horizontal strikes water with velocity from a height of fifteen feet, it is said to be akin to hitting concrete; all the breath is knocked out of you and your lungs refuse to work; you are about to suffocate.

That didn't matter in the case of Lance Corporal Miles Walcott of the Blues & Royals, for he was already dead.

The second mortar had scored a direct hit on the starboard side of the Southern Breeze. Dock workers splintered. On the hill to the north of the harbour and in the car park to the south, men hurried to reload and fire the mortar tubes protruding through the cut-away roofs of their vans. Two more mortars detonated, one outside the canteen, stoving in some windows, and one in the middle of the harbour water.

If one projectile had hit its target, it was a signal day for the South Armagh Active Service Unit of Defence Ireland, a.k.a. the Border Foxes. The spotter with binoculars on a balcony on Hill Street growled "That's it" into his walkie-talkie. The vans shortly drove off, avoiding wheelspin and drama. The thing about mortars is that they don't make much noise when they fire off, so it is hard to locate them.

(As an aside; a few days later, the Duke of Sussex, Baron Kilkeel, formerly of the Blues & Royals and the Household Cavalry, received a picture postcard from Kilkeel at Kensington Palace inviting him to 'drop in for tea sometime'. Signed 'Mick & the lads'. The police took it away.)

Those who hadn't fled the harbour crept out of hiding a safe time later. They knew the police would be coming. They went down to the Southern Breeze. One man was unconscious on the deck; there must be more below.

The deck was scattered with peculiar fishing gear where packing cases had cracked open – rifles, hand guns, bullet-proof jackets. One man found a dark beret with badge and insignia stating '*honi soit qui mal y pense*'. He slipped it into his pocket.

A docker shouted from the water's edge "Look, Look!" A body floating on the water. They cast off a row boat to salvage the body. Then the police arrived. There was five minutes of random chaos as facts were established, phoned in, ambulances called, people plodding around the deck.

A civilian 4-wheel drive screeched onto the dock; "Who's in charge?" Not a Northern Ireland accent, that's for sure. Two men got out and found the police officer directing operations. He was up to his knees assisting the row boat back to shore. The two men took him aside…"Nobody told me!"

Moments later, he summoned all the police; "Get all civilians out. All civilians out! Now! Drop everything. All civilians leave the dock!"

Gerald Ashton was having tea in his flat at Number Ten when he heard the news. "Jesus Christ!"

He hurried to the Ops Room only for the latest update to be confirmed; one dead, one critical, two in shock, one unaccounted for.

"Unaccounted for?" In a ferocious whisper, "What the fuck does that mean?"

"The officer controlling the Op, Captain Harris... Can't find him."

"Jesus. Dredge the harbour."

The five-o'clock news that day reported a terrorist bomb had gone off prematurely killing the terrorist and injuring two fishermen. The terrorist's body had been retrieved from the harbour by dock workers before the arrival of the emergency services. The whole area is now in lockdown.

Political parties from all sides were quick to bemoan the outrage. A unionist councillor in Belfast trumpeted "You were told over and over. The IRA has not gone away. The Good Friday Agreement is a sham." No one could explain why the IRA would want to bomb a fishing boat in an area where over half the workers were catholic.

The Prime Minister had read the brief; some joker had been incinerated in a fire on the morning a protestant farm near Banbridge had been torched. It was being put down to catholic land agitators.

On the afternoon of the fire, a porter at the hospital had seen this guy Sweeney admitted and rushed to surgery. The ambulance driver whispered he had been pulled out of a barn, half dead, near Keady. Bandit country. He phoned the cops. Sweeney had form; suspected IRA; convictions for… cattle rustling. Good God! Obviously incompetent, but worth keeping an eye on. His 'friends' would be coming to visit.

The dock worker who had pocketed the military beret went to meet his mates for a pint that evening in a state of anticipation. One of his mates seemed particularly familiar with military insignia and was pleased to take the beret into his care.

The following morning being a Saturday, the news channels were struggling for copy other than sports previews. The news broke on the 11 o'clock bulletin from Belfast and was immediately taken up by London, and everywhere else.

The Taoiseach in Dublin was ripping mad and wouldn't take his call. The civil servant at Downing Street apologised profusely while speculating that there must be a mistake. To his knowledge, there were no active members of the Blues and Royals in Northern Ireland at present.

"So who owns the beret and the military ordnance in Kilkeel harbour? Which port do these so-called fishermen operate out of?"

Among the many trying to get through to the PM was Billy McKay MP. He was livid as well. He wanted to know who had leaked the mission so that anti-British elements could prepare an ambush.

Sinn Fein released a statement saying they had forsworn violence as per the terms of the Good Friday Agreement.

A spokeswoman for The Movement said "This barely credible disaster shows why Ireland must control its own affairs.

Foreigners have once again tried to interfere, with predictable results." End of statement.

The dead and injured were taken in an unmarked lorry to hospital in Newry, followed by the two men in a 4x4 and several blacked-out SUVs; past Warrenpoint, past Narrow Water where eighteen men of the 2nd Paratroop regiment had paid Soldiers' Dues in August '79, past the Newry Canal where Fonsie Sweeney had learned to swim, past the ford where Cú Chullain, the Hound of Ulster, had defeated Ferdia, the hero of Connacht, in battle over the Brown Bull of Cooley.

And so to Daisy Hill where they could observe Fonsie Sweeney, swathed in bandages and morphine, at close quarters.

The Adjutant General of the Blues & Royals was incandescent with rage and embarrassment. Not only had a simple operation become a complete cock-up, but they couldn't find one of his soldiers, and his regiment was the personal bodyguard of the king. He'd have to stand down! An immediate internal enquiry was ordered.

The Taoiseach knew this state of affairs could not continue. If the country was to be at the mercy of marauding Whiteboys and with this group, The Movement, offering a radical Third Way in politics, he could lose control. He was hearing they were organising a major parade in Dublin in July. He called the respected Senator D'Arcy to get a reading on cross-party opinion.

CHAPTER 8

The red-haired girl was certainly attractive. She kept the patrons of the King & Castle amused with a cheeky line in conversation but always accompanied by a smile. The middle-aged men, sore from the correctness of the office, were pleased with the attention and the chance for a little off-colour chat without being reprimanded by some brainless toad of an eighteen-year-old office drone.

She was Saoirse. Some of them struggled (deliberately) with the pronunciation, so a compromise was reached; Sally. She didn't mind. Sally was a nice name.

Her brother was a professional footballer; played in the Championship division in West London. She was over here to 'mind him', she said. And he was a decent player; solid if not spectacular. Some way to go for an international call-up, but who knows?

The lads came in regularly from the barracks. "Chelsea! Chelsea!" they'd chant, just to annoy her, for they played in blue as well. On Saturday evenings, after the day's league fixtures, there was always plenty of sledging, or 'slagging' as she called it. They usually had a few too many and had to be shown the door at drinking-up time. The locals called them the Booze and Royals.

Mark was different. He had quietly fallen for her when she first arrived two years ago. Everyone knew, but nothing much was said except for the odd wolf whistle when he stayed on while the rest were ejected. For he was a Corporal. Footie rivalry was fine, but his private life was strictly off-limits.

Attraction is a funny thing. There's nothing pretty about iron filings but they congregate to a magnet. Mark wasn't pretty either; thick glasses, slightly puffy face, bald patch on top; generally quite round, in fact. The type of man whose mind is easily separated from his appearance as there seemed to be little correlation between them. But he was sharp, hence the rank. His forte was mathematics and logistics.

They hit it off from the outset. Whether she admired him for his mind or saw in him less competition from other women didn't matter. His mates could see only the oddest of matches. Being a country girl with brothers, she already knew gold could be mined in the most unlikely seams.

He treated her well. Nothing fancy – nice dinners every now and then, a text at night to say Sweet Dreams, a guided tour of the stables at Buckingham Palace ('Buck House') to see the horses and the state carriages.

And they didn't even understand each other all the time, he being a 'Geordie' (Newcastle) and she being a 'Jack' (Dublin). And, of course, that became their furtive moniker in the ranks; 'Jack & Geordie'.

To her he was non-threatening, pleasant and great chat. In fact, he used to go on a bit once he got started. Compared to his belted and buckled life in the army, she was easy company. He once told her he had told her more about himself than he had ever told anyone.

Then he added that was because she was remote from him, but trusted, his life story would not come back to haunt him. While they were great friends, he couldn't see a long-term future for them. Some James Bond-type would come along and sweep her up.

She appeared stung about that initially, perhaps because she thought they were somewhat closer than 'remote', and for a few days she was quieter, and he could see it. He didn't want to lose her; "Hey, I'm over your way next week".

"Where, Dublin?"

"Noo, noo. Northern Ireland. As British as Newcastle, I'm told."

"I don't know the North much. Never actually been there."

"The lads say it's OK now the troubles are over."

"I thought the soldiers were all gone from there."

"Most are. Just the odd little recce. There's still a few bad guys around."

"I think it's sad. It's a pity people can't live together."

He smiled, and they moved on.

This attack on Captain Butchart-Grimley - though it took place in the physical north of the island - it was in the South, politically. That's just the way the border ran. When it was first set up in 1922, the border was engineered to protect British hegemony in Northern Ireland by ensuring a loyal protestant/unionist majority, regardless of geography.

Senator D'Arcy knew the party leaders would be worried about the same things as he – reprisal raids – which could mean loyalist incursions over the border and a rebirth of the IRA in retaliation. He asked all party political leaders and deputy leaders to meet two days hence. In the meantime, he would gauge opinion in the North.

The nationalist population in the North was in high dudgeon. What were the British doing, trying to sneak an undercover unit into Northern Ireland when the place was on a political knife edge?

The PSNI were indignant; this was their territory. They'd been trying to build trust for years. This could set back the peace process disastrously.

The Secretary of State for Northern Ireland was in London, seeking clarification.

Turlough O'Toole engaged his shocked customers as best he could. Condemnation and sympathy were exchanged in sad whispers. And all the time, he waited for the telephone call he knew must come.

He had tried, fairly successfully, to put Father Tomás Doherty out of his mind. He was locked up in his secure hospital, quietly waiting to be vindicated. He could afford to wait. He was at peace. He had struck a great blow – his life's work. But more than that, he had given Ireland security for the future. Free at last! He had only to depend on the policeman...

By midday, no phone call had come. The sword of Damocles remained sheathed. At 3 in the afternoon, a courier arrived bearing gifts; marked private & personal; a CD, secondhand, for the cover wrapping had been removed. The music was Isao

Tomita's Debussy, extruded through a synthesiser. Very worthy, certainly, and very old. Included in the sleeve notes, a slip of paper with a telephone number.

O'Toole excused himself and walked to the mini-market where there was a phone; the town's last remaining payphone. All the rest had been irrevocably vandalised. On the third ring DD answered "Hiya?"

"Busy."

"I'm sure you are. Would you like to meet for a chat?"

"When?"

"This evening."

"Where?"

"You know Assaroe Lake, between Belleek and Ballyshannon? There's a fishing lodge two miles out of Ballyshannon on the N3. See you there at seven."

The last time O'Toole had agreed to an isolated venue suggested by DD, it was the Hell Fire Club, two years ago, and that hadn't gone so well.

"Very isolated."

"Yea, and I'll explain why. I can't say much. This is a pay-as-you-go phone. I won't use this number again. Bring the letter."

O'Toole hesitated. The letter. He never wanted to open the letter.

"Bring the letter," she emphasised. The phone went dead. That was that, then. The letter. Game on.

O'Toole wasn't the type of man to involve others. He had some sort of faith in himself and wanted to see things through by himself. It wasn't hubris, he believed, it was self-reliance, the same self-reliance that caused him to go alone to meet a mass-murderer at the Hell Fire Club when he could have taken half the police in Dublin with him and arrested The Druid and saved everybody a lot of trouble.

Now he was going to meet a woman who certainly was implicated, though he didn't know how far or even what her intentions were, except a United Ireland. A noble goal, but by what methods? Other activists looking at him would see not a scrupulous, torn individual but a plodding foot soldier, a martyr, embedded for the cause. There was no way of backing out and he didn't fancy his kneecaps being blown off. He phoned Maire.

He had to tell Maire something, so he told her he was going to meet an associate in Belleek. And as he was celebrating a completely fictional monthly sales record in the shop, might he stop by at 9 pm with a bottle of red to celebrate the occasion? He knew she'd be sure he'd never break an appointment without letting her know.

At 6:30, he set off for Belleek, the letter in the ripped lining of his riding chaps; just in case. Driving down the M3, he found himself constantly glancing in the mirror. Paranoid? He knew they had watched him for at least a year after The Druid debacle. They knew where to find him, hiding out in Belize, and the CIA was in on it too. Now that he was in plain sight, was he still of interest to them?

Was DD being watched? Undoubtedly. Though she wasn't given to regular public statements, she was evidently a prominent figure in The Movement. And though it was a legitimate enterprise, it had the capacity to upset a lot of applecarts, so vested interests would be protecting their turf – using all the available assets of the state.

He pulled in at the fishing lodge. It was a fine, warm evening; lots of flies, so the fish would be rising. People with various classes of fishing gear were flitting about. He sat for a minute, remembering the cold, dark Halloween morning he had gone with a gun in his pocket to meet The Druid and the intimidating Alphonsus Sweeney. Then she was there.

She embraced him and a kiss on either cheek. If there were long-distance photographers, it might as well look natural (but not too intimate). They set off towards the woods, discussing the weather and the drive down. Into the woods, where the profusion of trees would foil any long-distance microphones. They ambled along easily, no particular destination in view.

"You've followed the fallout from Kilkeel?"

"Yes, it was quite a mess. Have they found the missing soldier?"

"Apparently they found an epaulette from his fatigues. No sign of him. They think he was eviscerated by a direct hit."

"Can that happen?"

"Apparently it can; you're just blown to small bits."

"Jesus!"

"Did you hear Ashton on the radio this morning? Denies all knowledge."

"Yea."

"It's heaven sent. Now we can send him a little reminder."

O'Toole said nothing. He just stared ahead; it was a form of assent, of resignation, of the inevitable. She was looking round, looking for anyone in front or behind. They took a barely-beaten track, parallel to the water's edge, and happened upon an uprooted tree trunk where they sat down. The sun was still bright above the tree line, pleasant shafts of light darting in and out of the leaves. She opened her handbag and took out a packet of cigarettes, an old-time butane lighter and a vial of lighter fuel. She didn't smoke.

"Have you made a copy?"

"Huh*?*"

"… of the letter?"

"No."

She flicked the lighter. "This is just in case we have company."

With an uncontrollable sadness, as if he were about to read his own Will, he withdrew the envelope from an inside pocket. '*To be opened only in the event of my death.*' A firm hand. Obviously not The Druid's, for he was too unwell at the time this letter would have been written. He handed it to DD.

She took a nail file from her bag and, making sure she wasn't cutting the paper inside, began to saw along the seal. She extracted a folded-over sheet of white A4. There was no salutation, no address, no date, no signature.

There was five short lines of 12-point text in the middle of the page. She scanned them and handed the paper to him.

It was the end of May and a heat haze hung stubbornly over the Weald of Kent. Students milled about with the appearance of heightened sensitivity for it was exams time and within the hour they would experience the terror and excitement that comes with being isolated in a crammed exam hall and someone calls out "You may open your examination papers".

At 9:30am exactly, hundreds of pairs of hands broke the seals and eyes scanned the questions. Those who had studied correctly relaxed and began methodically at Question One; the others, in a maelstrom of regret, hunted for the questions they thought they knew the answers to and quickly calculated the odds of success.

The hum of the air conditioning and the flight of an errant fly provided a distraction for those consumed with misgiving as they realised they had opted for the wrong king; it was Henry V, not Richard III.

At three minutes to ten, the door of the Exams Hall sprung open with indecent urgency and the vice-principal hurried to the front of the room. Without preamble he announced in a ringing voice "Everyone, leave your examination papers and go directly to the fire assembly station. Now!" The fire alarm sounded.

Incomprehension,

"Leave your exam papers, your computers and your school bags and go now, to the assembly point in the front quad." He marched to the nearest student and whipped the computer mouse from his hand. Realisation. Students and invigilators rose noisily and hastened in a crush towards the door. "Don't push!"

Down the stairs to where they were met by a line of uniformed police and soldiers. Pushing up the stairs, three people in biohazard suits."To the fire assembly area!"

At the Fire Assembly, more police and Mr. Saddler, head of Facilities. "All gather here, please." The students and staff, faces changing from enquiry to shock. "Is everyone here? Listen, *listen*! We are now going to walk quietly to the playing fields. No running. Behind me, please." Mr Saddler set off at a brisk pace followed by huddles of students seeking their friends for company, marshalled by unsmiling police.

"What's wrong sir? What's wrong?"

The procession marched towards where the heat haze had been in the playing fields, the lakes and the Medway. A policeman shouted "Keep walking." Over the playing fields, past the Sailing Club, towards Haysden, now a procession of the fearful.

"What's wrong, Mr. Saddler?"

"I don't know, boys. We are under the direction of the police. Please, stay together."

In the Quad, the vice-principal was in urgent conversation with police officers and an army sergeant; "I can only confirm, sir, what we told you earlier. We have reliable information that a toxic bacterial agent has been hidden somewhere on the school grounds and could be released at any time. That's all we know. The whole school will have to be searched." More vehicles arrived and bio-hazard suits deployed.

Further afield, police and army roadblocks were being set up. The A21 was closed. Emergency news announcements: "Avoid Tonbridge."

Interest, concern, apprehension and then worry. The word was on the street; Chipping Norton! Then the helicopters started to sweep in.

By 11am, twenty thousand people were running, stumbling, pushing to their cars, their bicycles, their boats. Some locked their premises, some tried to phone an ambulance, some carried their dogs, cats in baskets. Some stood frozen in the street and cried; some didn't understand. "Why?"

"Help me. My mother is ill. She can't move."

By 11:30, all roads, streets and phone circuits were grid-locked. Servers crashed. Police cars were stuck in the local station. People ran towards the open fields, the ridge, the river, the woods, and the railway station, only to find that two drivers had fled their trains outside the station, blocking the lines.

One man who had been prepared for the end of days since Chernobyl walked to his basement feeling vindicated, grabbed a pannier with tinned food, an am/fm radio, batteries, torchlight, a spare mobile phone, and a pistol, fixed the pannier to his trail bike, and took the shortest route to high ground. He had seen the apocalypse movies.

At 1pm, the Prime Minister came on the television and declared a national emergency.

In Broadmoor Hospital for the Criminally Insane, Father Tomás Doherty, known as The Druid, asked to be taken to the prison chapel so he could pray.

At Combermere Camp in Berkshire, The Blues and Royals were mobilised and an armoured detachment sped the short distance to Windsor Castle where the king was in residence.

With the deployment of The Sanctuary Knocker threat in Tonbridge, all activity seemed to be suspended by gossamer threads on the neighbouring islands of Britain and Ireland, unless one was caught up in the immediate blizzard, in which case one's life had become uncontrolled chaos and desperation. Such are the necessary consequences of war.

Those who were in the immediate line of fire – civil servants and bureaucrats – tried to maintain communications and make sense out of what had happened. Politicians on either side of the Irish Sea were mute, lest they make the situation worse and provoke the next visitation of the amoeba.

Senior politicians sent forth spokesmen who spoke of international cooperation in the face of evil. In the bookshop in Bundoran, the bookseller sold his books with the barest of prologue or epilogue lest he thread on fractured nerves.

Five days later, The Movement announced a monster parade in Dublin.

For over one hundred years, the Irish Republic had steered a very cautious course between rhetoric and reality in its dealings with its own citizens in Northern Ireland.

Under Article 3 of the Irish Constitution written in 1937 by the old nationalist Eamon DeValera, the island of Ireland could aspire to unity of the national territory. When lectured by Unionists that this was not a very *communitaire* stance, and unhelpful in fostering good relations with unionists in a modern Europe, the people of the Irish Republic were only too glad to sacrifice the aspiration in the same way as they were willing to sacrifice their fellow countrymen in the North who were getting it in the neck from the cornerboys of the British army from 1972 onwards.

At the request of the Taoiseach, Senator D'Arcy had canvassed opinion of the other parties. They were of one mind, if for different reasons; this 'Movement' for uniting Ireland was trouble. A Garda officer had been injured at the GPO during their last march in Dublin and the Gardai at large, it was rumoured, were keen to 'have a go' at them. It didn't matter if they were non-party-political or not.

It is the nature of the Irish Gardai to be fairly 'thick', as in 'uncompromising', a tradition of peace-keeping and peace-making going back to the famous Irish-American general 'Fighting Phil' Sheridan who is credited with the doctrine "The only good Indian is a dead Indian" during the winning of The West.

Sinn Fein, for their part, were not anxious to promote a group which might steal their constituency.

The other political parties did the mathematics, and saw their parliamentary representation in a 32-county united Ireland significantly diminished.

Besides, this 'Movement' was obviously in league with marauding Whiteboys and, it is rumoured, possibly associated with the Anthrax weapon. Certainly Father Tomás Doherty, directly implicated in the Anthrax attack, was a spiritual mentor to The Movement.

Those with eyes to see now saw the significance of the Tonbridge crisis – the British could no longer adventure in Ireland for fear of instant retribution. The Sanctuary Knocker defence effectively allowed Ireland to pursue its own destiny and solve its own problems unmolested from without.

Now the only question was; would the guardians of The Sanctuary Knocker threaten its use in Ireland? Senator D'Arcy decided to go for a walk.

Although he liked to get out of the confines of Dail Eireann occasionally, he was aware that, once outside the guarded portals,

The Sanctuary Knocker

he would be the target of every crank, deviant and constituent in the country. Ireland is a small town; all public representatives are readily recognised. So he avoided St Stephens Green which would be thick with office workers and tourists enjoying the sun and walked instead to the playing fields at the back of Trinity College where he could hope to go undisturbed.

His first priority must be to secure his farm. Given the history of 'Irregular' marauders in Roscommon during the War of Independence and his own public profile, it was not out of order to think he could be a target. So he would have to give one of the cottages on the farm to a full-time watchman-cum-tractor driver. There was probably some subvention available to the Father of The House for personal security; he'd check that. Plus a regular Garda patrol.

Second, a coordinated response to the Movement parade. At this stage, there are no grounds for cancelling it. Current intel on the leadership shows no unlawful political involvement. But certainly a step-up in security all round. Keep an eye on that bookshop in Bundoran; let the PSNI watch McAdam and that woman in Derry. The warning about Tonbridge had come from an English voice, a public call box in Essex in England, a recognised codeword. So this lot are organised. Best thing to do is invite them in for a cup of tea and a chat. Maybe we'll find out something.

Third, the Gardai. They're looking for a fight after that detective Devlin got thumped in O'Connell Street. Have to keep a lid on that. Could end up with a reputation like the RUC in the seventies.

He stopped for a minute to watch the rugby practice. Get Sinn Fein on board. Might have to give them a seat on the Civil Emergencies sub-committee. But that would mean giving them access to a Cabinet security briefing...

The rugby ball bounced rudely close to him, but he resisted the urge to throw it back. A weedy youth rushed past to collect. Yes, good idea to invite them for a chat; give them a chance to see him on their side; for the good of the country, don't you know.

CHAPTER 9

"Here is the news…

"Berkshire police have today arrested a woman in Windsor on suspicion of passing confidential military information to a hostile agent. It is understood the 23-year old woman is a foreign national.
Military sources have also revealed that a Corporal in the Blues and Royals, one of the most senior regiments in the British Army, based in Combermere Barracks in Windsor, is under military arrest on suspicion of disclosing secret information on military operational matters.
No further information is available at this time."

A junior minister from the government, whose constituency happened to be adjacent, arrived in a car, using the helicopters in the sky above Tonbridge to pinpoint the epicentre of the event. His concern was any evidence of a crop-duster plane circling the town. The most awful of prospects – this scare was induced in order to get thousands of people away from cover and onto the streets where they would be as children against the deadly Anthrax spray.

He immediately made contact with the head of military operations and established a communications line direct to the Prime Minister's office. Any argument about whether to keep people locked in their houses and businesses or herded on to the streets was now redundant.

Two lines of soldiers and police were seen to assemble at the junction of the B245 Sevenoaks Road and Shipbourne Road, just beside the stricken school. One line moved north, stretching and contracting to take in every side street and alleyway. Knocking doors, climbing fences, ploughing across gardens to ensure that people had heard the warnings and were moving out with all speed.

The second line moved south, infiltrating Lansdowne Road, Bordyke, The Slade, The Angel. People were pushed ahead of the line, roused from their beds, ejected from their cars – "temporary inconvenience, sorry sir" – denied their pints in the pubs, half-dressed from the swimming pool, until a bemused, truculent glut of humanity, like the Children of Israel fleeing Egypt, arrived at the Bidborough Ridge where they rested, and were supplied with water, food, medical care and comfort from army trucks and ambulances. No one knew what would happen next.

Inside the school, operatives moved from room to room seeking anything, any container, atomiser, air conditioner or pressurised vessel that might release a spray or cause contamination. Everything suspect was carried to specialised lorries with airtight enclosures. Fire extinguishers were deposited in transparent boxes equipped with chemical sniffers to determine the contents. Giant trucks with cannons to spray formaldehyde were lined up in Hildenborough and Southborough. Much had been learned from Oxford.

By 3pm, five hours after the warning, nothing had been found. Police were now in a quandary; Was it a hoax? Had they missed something? When to give the 'all clear'? The country fretted. International media waited. The thousands on the Bidborough Ridge, now tremulous and fractious, looked down in fear and panic upon their homes.

At ten past four, a phone rang in the Home Office. A member of the Emergency Committee answered. A password was spoken. The minister came to the phone; "This is His Majesty's Minister for Home Affairs." Techies switched on tracers and recorders.

"Minister..," an educated voice. "As our objective has now been achieved, I am prepared to tell you where to find The Sanctuary Knocker at Tonbridge School. I can assure you it is the only sample there and once it is decommissioned, the people of Tonbridge may return to their homes." He was reading from a script.

"Yes?"

Biohazard suits and security personnel hurried to the Boathouse. The students who had earlier fled to the lakes had long dispersed. Armed military approached the door; boobytrap drill.

Once inside, military scientists zoned in on three fire extinguishers. They had all been replaced last year, after Chipping Norton. Two red, one grey. Each had a fine layer of dust, but the red ones bore seals showing service dates. The grey extinguisher had no seal. Records showed there had not been a fire in the boathouse in recent memory.

A helicopter landed on the playing fields, received the three extinguishers and transported them to a heavily guarded mobile laboratory parked in a quarry three miles away. Within an hour, the grey extinguisher revealed its secret. The threat was real.

A detective team, led by Inspector Alf Scouse from Scotland Yard, a veteran of Irish-terror operations, arrived to interview staff. The Boathouse, he was told, was generally open. Anyone could have planted the bacteria. The area was popular with walkers.

Kitchen staff remembered an affable Irish chap who used to deliver the meat three times a week. Talked about rugby all the time. Chef used to give him a doughnut to have with his coffee.

The voice recording from the minister's conversation was checked by GCHQ at Cheltenham. It showed this was the same caller who had made a suspicious call to the Jimmy Youngman radio phone-in programme two years ago, warning of terrorist attacks.

Two detective Gardai from the anti-terror squad arrived up from Dublin to investigate the arson attack on Captain Butchart-Grimley. The lads from Ballyshannon station had already sealed off the farm and had completed a sweep of the land. Nothing specific had been found.

The Captain lived alone, except for the housekeeper who came in two days a week to tidy and cook his meals. She was not present on the day in question. The Captain hadn't heard or seen anything unusual during the night. Obviously they came on foot, and in this quiet rural location, could have parked a getaway vehicle anywhere.

Next job was to interview the neighbours. Mrs. O'Donnell, an elderly widow woman who had a bungalow 100 yards down the road, couldn't be of any help.

The next farm was the small equestrian centre belonging to Maire ni Raighbheartaigh, the well-known musician. Like all good detectives, the Dublin men had made some basic enquiries before leaving the capital and were rewarded with an intriguing connection between the second violin of the symphony orchestra and the manager of the Main Street Bookshop in Bundoran, one Turlough O'Toole, late of the Garda Siochana, Harcourt Street, Dublin.

Former Inspector O'Toole, having fled the jurisdiction after the fractious 'Druid' hearings, had returned and had, apparently, gone political. Most interestingly, his tail reported active participation in The Movement, including making a fairly anodyne speech at The Movement parade in Eyre Square, Galway in October last.

He was photographed with Ms. ni Raighbheartaigh at musical evenings in Sligo and Donegal and they had dined out on a number of occasions, always returning to their own homes at the end of the evening. Ms. ni Raighbheartaigh was an accomplished violinist, very popular in the National Concert Hall, and a regular in the Society magazines in Dublin.

Other than this relationship, O'Toole kept a low profile except for one notable associate, Doreen Downey.

Known widely as 'DD', she has long been identified with radical political activity and has already been investigated for her association with some high-profile agitators including Fr. Tomás Doherty and Alphonsus Sweeney, a suspected IRA hitman. He is wanted for questioning in the Republic over the death of Cedric T Wall, First Secretary at the British Embassy two years ago, but has dropped out of sight. He is known to have escaped capture in England last year when a hijacked research ship, the W P Cupp, was bombed and sunk on the Thames by ultra-nationalist elements of the Royal Air Force. He was last seen in Neasden, North London.

It is known that O'Toole met him in the company of Downey in a pub in Derry two years ago and subsequently at the Hell Fire Club in the Dublin mountains.

Downey is an industrial chemist with the Zandtl Corporation of Germany. Her job means a lot of travelling to Munich and London. She is well regarded in her field.

Her father was a well-known dance band musician and played inter-county football for Derry. So she would have been raised in a Gaelic household. This does not directly translate to extreme nationalist sympathies, but it is a short distance from cultural immersion to radical expression. She is known to have taken an active part in the celebrations for the anniversary of the Easter Rising which could account for her association with some of the suspect individuals noted above.

As it is stated policy within the Force to keep an eye on *all* radicals, we will continue to monitor her activities.

Maire ni Raighbheartaigh was outgoing and helpful. She invited them to have tea and biscuits; they both had glasses of water. She recognised the difficult position the Captain was in for he most assuredly looked upon Ireland as his home. The country had been good to him and he felt happy, obliged even, to reciprocate. He knew the neighbours did occasionally make fun of his colonial mannerisms, but it was done in good humour and without malice. He had sponsored a trophy for Best Bullock at the Donegal Town fair and it was a sought-after prize. In her opinion, any attack upon the Captain was entirely political and took no account of his standing as a gentleman, which made her feel even greater regret over the incident.

The detectives thanked her profusely and as they, no less than others, were struck by her charm and dignity, rather mumbled their uncertain way out the door. Next stop, Mr. O'Toole.

It is said that a man's character comes to the fore *in extremis*. Despite the Fates conspiring mightily against him, O'Toole had been, after all, a Detective Inspector in the Garda Siochana.

So when he had been called upon to face his inquisitors two years previously at the '*O'Rourke Tribunal on Garda Practice,*

Procedure and Promotion within the State (With Particular Reference to Activities Surrounding the Recent Death of Mr. Cedric T. Wall and Others)', and risked public disgrace, he came out fighting and took on the Prosecution in a manner which earned him plaudits in the media. He was subsequently allowed to resign.

And a year later, when he was forced to travel from his purgatory in Belize, he scattered the Star Chamber in London with defiance and rebuttal as a man should do.

So he was well able to defend himself. The two detectives were aware of this and would approach this questioning with respect. There was no reason for O'Toole to talk to them at all, but he was a free man, a reborn man with little to hide except, perhaps, a letter. So he agreed to meet them in the flat above the shop. If it was already bugged, it would save them the bother.

They were just there to find out anything that could help to further their search for the captain's attackers. In the course of their conversation, it remained unsaid that O'Toole had spoken in public on behalf of The Movement and some people were making a connection between The Movement and the rise of the Whiteboys.

The detectives thanked O'Toole for seeing them and were genuine in their contention that his actions in The Druid case, which led to his downfall, would not have been taken by a lesser man.

O'Toole thanked them for their words of comfort and sent his fraternal greetings back to the men and women in the Force. He specifically asked them to wish a speedy recovery to Gard Devlin who had once been his assistant, and who had been injured at the Dublin parade.

As to the Captain; he knew him as a customer and as a friend and neighbour of Ms. ni Raighbheartaigh ("who, as you know, is *my* very good friend"), and as an honourable and upstanding man. O'Toole was not aware of any activity on the part of the captain that would single him out for the attention of Whiteboys.

He was also concerned that spontaneous public reaction to the fire was that it was the work of Whiteboys as opposed to, for example, a jealous neighbour or disgruntled relative. The detectives were pleased to agree with this caution which was only to be expected, they said, from a man who had long and hard experience in criminal investigation. They parted on convivial terms.

The following is an extract from the case notes arising from a visit by two members of the PSNI to the residence of Mrs. Doreen Downey (née Reynolds) at her home in Derry/Londonderry on 3rd. July this year.
The visit was at the request of the Garda Siochana, Harcourt Street, Dublin. The meeting was held in the study of Mrs. Downey's home.
Present were Mrs. Downey, Sgt Albert Crozier & Sgt Patrick Finnegan of PSNI and Inspector Desmond Hanna of SDU Division, Garda Siochana, Phoenix Park, Dublin (auditing). Inspector Hanna has worked with former Det. Insp. Turlough O'Toole in the past :

"Mrs. Downey asked all to be seated. and immediately made a statement:

"I want to make it clear that I am a director of an organisation known as The Movement. The single purpose of this organisation is to expedite the abolition of any border in Ireland, be it physical, political or philosophical. In pursuit of this aim, all inhabitants and citizens of the island of Ireland will be expected to give their undivided allegiance to Ireland and to Ireland only." Now gentlemen, you may continue with your agenda for this meeting... Oh, am I under arrest or under caution?"

Sgt Crozier replied:

"No, Mrs. Downey. We are here simply in pursuit of our enquiries, at the request of the Garda Siochana, into a suspected arson attack on a farm near Bundoran two days ago. We have no information that you were in any way complicit in this incident, but we are trying to establish if your organisation, 'The Movement', is in any way connected to this or other recent arson attacks."

Mrs. Downey: "And how would you propose to establish that?"

Sgt Crozier: "By simply asking you as a responsible and prominent citizen in the community if there is any such link."

Mrs. Downey: "And they sent three of you to do that?" Silence.

Sgt Crozier: "Mrs. Downey, you were interviewed by the PSNI eighteen months ago concerning your relationship with Inspector Turlough O'Toole of the Garda Siochana in regards to what is known as *The Druid* case..?"

Mrs. Downey: "Yes."

Sgt Crozier: "And during that interview it was established that you had associations with various members of organisations known to be engaged in criminal activity."

Mrs. Downey: "Do you mean IRA volunteers?"

Sgt Crozier: "Yes I do."

Mrs. Downey: "Well, we'd better get our terms of references clear. I look upon the IRA as freedom fighters. What they do in their spare time is no concern of mine… at this time."

Sgt. Crozier: "The IRA is a proscribed organisation."

Mrs. Downey: "Is it indeed? And am I to be proscribed for giving them moral support in their battle to rid this country of any and all malevolent British influence?"

Sgt. Crozier: "There is no law against holding political opinions."

Mrs. Downey: "There is a new reality on this island and it is simply this; there will be a united Ireland. If you are caught on the wrong side of that argument, when the time comes, you had better make your arrangements. There will be no sympathy for you."

Sgt. Crozier: "That does not justify criminal activity."

Mrs. Downey: "The winners will be the judge of what is criminal activity and what isn't."

Sgt. Finnegan: "It seems to me you are sailing close to the wind, Mrs. Downey. I would have thought a lady in your position would do more to promote harmony in society."

Mrs. Downey: "Harmony is for musicians. Winning this is all…"

Sgt. Finnegan: "By any means?"

Mrs. Downey: "By any means."

Sgt. Crozier: "You have made your position clear, Mrs. Downey. I advise you not to speak in those terms in public as you could be liable under the Terrorism Act 2000 which is still in force. Good day."

End of Case Notes."

The three officers rose as one and, preceded by Doreen Downey, left the house without the formality of shaking hands.

Inspector Hanna (SDU Division) was impassive. As a man who liked to be on the side of the winners, he was taking careful note. Last to step off the pillared doorway, he inclined his head towards his hostess and whispered "This lark won't fly in the South " and she could see only disdain in his face. Her card was well marked.

Hanna was an interesting man; smarmy, vicious, controlled. He had worked with O'Toole on the very political Cedric T. Wall case. His air of superiority, even with his superiors, suited him to the political side of the Gardai Special Detective Unit (SDU) based in the Phoenix Park. He left the footwork of criminal investigation to clod-hoppers like O'Toole while he turned his talents to the more *cerebral* aspects of terrorist behaviour such as free speech, right of assembly, and insurrection.

And he'd be damned if he would let this bunch of creeping anarchists take over the island. He liked a serene life; gated communities, better dining (in select company, of course), purring autos; oh, and good shirts.

He found shirts that creased at the collar most irritating, so he brought his shirts in from France. An indulgence, certainly, but a satisfying one, and easily enough financed through his extra-mural activities and *business* connections.

It was quite logical really; an organised, structured underworld element using a single point of contact which could be trusted to discourage and dispose of the low-life type of criminal upstart who left needles lying about and was a drain on the Legal Aid budget. And besides, the Godfathers afforded him some peace of mind and protection, you might say, in difficult situations.

He was pleased with the opportunity to audit the discussion with Mrs. Downey. Now it was time to have a chat with the Senator…

The Senator was busy. There was a pregnant woman stuck in quarantine at Birmingham airport and the balloon was about to go up.

Patricia and Gerry Ferriter had been at church on London Road on the morning the crop sprayer plane had launched its Anthrax attack on Chipping Norton. They had risen from their pews at the end of 11 o'clock Mass to find the door of the church closed and their exit barred by a uniformed police officer. He called out: "Will you all stay in your place, please!" A harsh sound in a church.

He marched up the aisle to be met by the officiating priest Father Kearney who was completely taken aback. The policeman took him aside and after a heated conversation Father Kearney addressed his congregation: "My friends, apparently there has been a release of a harmful gas in the town during our celebration of the Mass. The police have asked us to remain in the church with the doors and windows closed until they can assess the severity of this, eh, incident. I think we should comply with this request despite the obvious inconvenience." Gasps and mumbling.

"What about my family at home?"

"My boy is at the Lido!"

The priest appealed for calm: "Apparently police officers have been deployed throughout the town to get people indoors. Try not to worry. If you have mobile phones, please feel free to use them to contact your families." A flurry of searching and dialing. The police officer asked the priest if he could remain in church with them. "Certainly."

The officer called his base to report the church secure. "Standby."

There was no food, but the toilet in the sacristy was made available to all. Several parishioners had small bottles of water and these were shared as far as they would go. Some men were content to drink from the baptismal font. Children were taken aside and formed into groups where they were read to from The Acts of the Apostles and the parish social magazine. Some people stretched out in the pews and tried to sleep.

During the interminable afternoon, some followed the local news on their phones until the batteries gave out. Apparently a small plane had flown over the town spraying a mist or foam of some sort. Mr. Bertie Clarkson, editor of the Cotswold Examiner, whom some of the parishioners knew, had received a phone call prior to the flight warning of a terrorist Anthrax attack!

Upon hearing this news, some parishioners began to shriek and cry; some cursed, then excused themselves. Father Kearney called upon all to come to the Lady altar where prayers would be offered up for their deliverance and for the people of the town. At no stage did anyone try to escape from the church.

At 5.15, the officer's radio whistled and, following a cryptic exchange with base, he and the priest walked to the altar steps and announced that the doors were now to be opened, and people should go straight home if they did not have to divert elsewhere.

Officer Taylor then gave them an Emergency number to call for queries about family members or friends.

Stepping outside, they found more police, and people in an agitated state. Patricia and Gerry drove straight home to Burford Road, tuning into local radio as they went. The station was broadcasting emergency messages from the Oxfordshire constabulary telling listeners to remain in their homes with doors and windows sealed.

On Monday evening, Pat and Gerry packed bags, locked the house, and drove to Gerry's brother Greg at the pub in Coalville. There they stayed inside the flat above the pub and waited for symptoms to appear while following all the news bulletins. Greg was worried about 'catching something', so he moved downstairs to the pub with a sleeping bag.

For days they monitored the news and medical bulletins, and kept in touch with the government emergency service. Greg left food, wine and water at their door. They felt like prisoners, only opening the door when he had gone away to take in the groceries, then closing it again. Much time was spent on the phone trying to placate and reassure their families and friends

After a week of isolation, there was no evidence of symptoms so they made arrangements to move again, this time to Patricia's aunt who owned a boarding house in Sutton Coldfield near Birmingham. They were glad to get out to see the rest of humanity again and, truth be told, Greg was glad to get his flat back.

But Patricia and Gerry were young and happily married and during their week of confinement, nature had taken its course…

Irish citizen detained at Birmingham airport.
Suspected of being carrier of Anthrax bacteria.

'Mrs. Patricia Ferriter, 26, a native of Westport, Co. Mayo, was yesterday detained by Dept. of Health officials at Birmingham airport as she was about to take a flight to Knock.

Mrs. Ferriter, who is eight months pregnant, is believed to be a victim of the infamous *Sanctuary Knocker* germ. Her late husband

Gerry, formerly of Mullingar, Co. Westmeath, died of Anthrax poisoning in March this year.

Mr. and Mrs. Ferriter had been resident in the Oxfordshire town of Chipping Norton when it was struck by an Anthrax attack last June. This attack was carried out at the instigation of the radical Irish priest Fr. Tomás Doherty who is serving a life sentence in England for his crimes.

The British Department of Health is of the opinion that this particular strain of Anthrax, codenamed Vollum 666, is believed to have been engineered in Russia, and can be transmitted by sexual intercourse like the human immunodeficiency virus, HIV.

A government spokesman in Dublin has said that while the government has the greatest sympathy for Mrs. Ferriter, it cannot allow her to land in Ireland and risk causing widespread infection until her status can be confirmed by extensive medical tests in England. Following her bereavement, Mrs. Ferriter had planned to return to live with her family in Westport.

A further characteristic of this bacterium is that it is potentially fatal only to humans with white skin. When questioned by reporters about the credibility of such a claim, a government scientist disagreed it was 'science fiction' and argued that Cancer Research UK, for example, has created a virus that targets and destroys cancer cells while leaving good cells alone. And cells are a constituent of the mechanism for controlling skin pigmentation.

He was not aware that the bacterium differentiates between nationalities, but affects all Caucasians equally.

Emergency questions have been scheduled for today's sitting of the Dail.'

It is said that the first mass migration of humanity occurred when humans spread out from the Great Rift Valley of Tanzania to inhabit the landmasses of Europe and Asia.

Millennia after that, millions of Irish called upon the charity of others and fled their famine-torn land in the 19th century to seek refuge in the New World.

The Africans returned in the early 21st century, seeking safe harbour and economic advance in the European nations. The Irish recognised a debt to be repaid and said 'Welcome', and the pristine, pale Irish were given a dash of contrast by black faces in Roscommon and Waterford and Dublin. Now, the charity of the Irish faced its greatest test.

Solutions were proposed from all quarters:

"Build a hospice at Keem Bay on Achill Island near her home in Mayo and let that be the redemption of the Famine village that used to exist there."
"It will become a leper colony."
"Isolate her in a hospital."
"What hospital? Who will have her?"
"What about the child?"
The pro-abortion lobby waded in; "Abort the child; it is a woman's right."
The Christian Sodality Group, joined by some Unionists: "The child is a gift of God."
"It is the devil's child."
The clergy were consulted: "All human life is sacred."
"What if the child is a monstrosity?"

And in the Dail;

"I don't know what this 'Movement' thinks it can achieve, but poisoning citizens is not the way to attract public support. I have it on good authority that this group will stop at nothing to achieve their aims."
"Nice to hear of some people who know what they want."
Calls for cancellation of the Dublin parade 'on public order grounds'.
"The Sanctuary Knocker is now the atom bomb of our age."

"This so-called priest is one of the biggest mass-murderers in the history of these islands."
"Furthermore, I also have it on the best authority that this group of so-called nationalists defaced our Irish flag two years ago at the Battle of the Boyne site in County Louth."

Mrs Ferriter was taken to a secure room in the airport normally reserved for interrogating terror suspects and deportees. An embassy representative was dispatched to provide comfort.

In his cell, the priest read The Passion of Christ.

The directors of The Movement ignored all the threats and jibes and instead trumpeted the success of the parade in Belfast, carried off without violence from any quarter. "A triumph for *all* the people of Ireland."
Publicity was increased for the Dublin parade, stoked by an announcement that it would be held on Sunday 13th July to allow people to attend their traditional Orange marches on 12th July and come to Dublin the following day.

CHAPTER 10

Three men sat in the upstairs room of a pub outside Dundalk, two bottles of spring water on the table. They were on important business; there would be no alcohol.

They were young, probably around twenty five, and fit looking; they looked like footballers.

Even with the door closed, they spoke in reserved tones, barely above a whisper. There was only one item on the agenda; how to get Fonsie out of the hospital.

He was a dangerous man, a soldier of *na Fianna*, and had a contrary way about him. So they weren't after him for his personality. They knew his history; if the state got him, he'd never see daylight again. But he got the job done. For that alone, he was worth bursting out.

What they knew was he was a suspect in the North and wanted in the South. So the chances are, he wouldn't be that heavily guarded in Newry. Joe Tomelty's daughter Margaret, who was a nurse in Oncology, said there was a PSNI man outside the door of the private ward, and two spooks down the corridor guarding the injured soldier from the Southern Breeze. They came and went for coffee, food and toilet at irregular intervals. Occasionally one would ask the other to 'keep an eye' while he took a break. As far as she knew, they all had hand guns.

Liam Maguire, leading the group, said there would be no gunfire in the hospital, so the guards had to be surprised and disabled. The easiest thing to do was to get somebody in dressed as a doctor; he or she would need a pass. Margaret could get one from the scrubs room during an operation, but they would have to work quickly because the pass would be reported missing and de-commissioned. The laundry van came on a Thursday; it was the oldest trick in the world, but it worked, if done right.

What are the odds they'd think anyone would want to burst Fonsie out? He'd been there for eleven days now, they might be more relaxed; and he'd be more able to travel. Margaret would draw up a detailed sketch of the corridor, exits, rooms, broom cupboards etc. They already knew the routes from the wards to the loading bays at the back and the ambulance set-down spaces at the front. They'd get two lads dressed as porters to put him in a laundry basket and take him down in the lift.

None of them had ever done anything like this before. The very thought made them nervous.

Obviously, Gerald Ashton could not continue at Number 10.

Beset by Chipping Norton and Tonbridge, he took his place at the Despatch Box and denied any connection to the Southern Breeze debacle. This did not cost him any misgivings; final victory for Gerald Ashton and Britain was all that mattered; any screw-up along the way was merely collateral damage.

Parliament was nearly convinced and he might have survived had intervention not arrived from an unexpected quarter. The previous day, a letter from the Regimental Colonel, Field Marshal Sir Ainsley Brand, of the Blues & Royals, had appeared in The Echo. It lamented the interference by certain politicians in the affairs of His Majesty's Armed Forces, in particular the Blues & Royals, who are a senior regiment and more importantly, part of the King's Bodyguard. *He* is their Colonel-in Chief.

Following a planned attack upon the king by a poisonous spider while attending Australian Independence Day celebrations two years ago, sensitivity to the inviolability of the Royal family had increased, courtiers had closed ranks and had sent the Sympathy machine into high gear, assuring the fealty of his subjects for another generation.

So that when Kensington Palace complained about this outrageous affront to Lord Kilkeel, a royal personage, it was too much for the Prime Minister's party and the Men in Grey Suits were sent forth with his execution warrant in hand.

There was no more time for inter-party wrangling; the state was in dire trouble from without. To focus resources and national goodwill, a government of National Unity was now necessary.

The senator had to be careful; he didn't want to overdress. This crowd might be the old Civil Rights types; builders, factory workers and tweedy teachers. She would be dressed; she can afford it.

He wanted them to believe he was on their side, that he'd mark their card. "We're all for a United Ireland. We're all in this together."

Hanna was a devious bastard, but he was right. This crowd was trouble. They had backing, they had organisation, and they were swaying unionist opinion, promising them the country. If it was their country, they'd make it in their own image! We're the natural parties of government; that would change with this lot charging around Dublin.

He'd have to take the initiative, control the meeting. He was an officer of the state, deserving of respect. His skills at appeasement were legendary.

He pulled up at the hotel; wall-to-wall weddings at the weekends; quieter today. He'd suggested using false names; "No need," she said.

Seventy-two now, but still fit. He adjusted his sober tie and got out of the car; quite sprightly. What was their picture of him? Well got, crafty, power-broker, fixer? The meeting was at eleven. He got there early; be in position, at ease.

The receptionist told him "The Drumlin Room, first floor." Nice hotel. They wouldn't come to Dublin, to his turf. Both sides away from home for this fixture.

He pushed the door. A woman and three men sitting round an oblong table, unsmiling. One free chair on the long side, for him. He was surrounded.

He moved forward to shake hands. Each made a perfunctory effort to rise.

"Robert McAdam, good morning."

"Doreen Downey. Thanks for coming."

"Packie Madden," and a nod of the head.

"Turlough O'Toole, good morning."

"Er… oh, good morning, Mr. O'Toole."

The table was spare; a jug of water and a tray of glasses in the centre. The senator looked about for instruments of conviviality. None. There was a water boiler on a side table, but no cups. He was dying for a coffee. You never have a meeting without coffee! And what was O'Toole doing here? He'd be questioned about the disposition of the Gardai. Jesus! They'd demand full protection for the parade. He couldn't guarantee what Hanna might be planning.

He'd read a précis of the case-notes; she was trouble. He didn't know Madden. McAdam would be straight.

"I'm glad to be able to meet you all, and I must say I'm very impressed with the conduct of your parades so far. Top class organisation, as far as I can see."

"Thank you, senator. Are you here on behalf of the government?" McAdam's question threw him.

"Em, well, em, I'm here with the blessing of the Taoiseach."

"Who is busy elsewhere, senator?" He could field Downey's sarcasm;

"This affair with Mrs. Ferriter is very sad. And between you and me, I can't see it being solved in the short term." Would they join him in the sympathy play?

"You won't let her into the country, will you? You don't want the problem."

"We're hoping to get a consensus."

"You won't get a consensus. She'll rot in England." If he was expecting the sympathy vote from that quarter, Mr. Madden had quickly disabused him.

"Senator d'Arcy, as you have said, we have run several parades to celebrate our country, and we have done it with the cooperation of the authorities and without trouble. Following recent remarks in the Dail can you, on behalf of the Taoiseach, guarantee us the full cooperation of the authorities, including the Gardai, for our parade on the thirteenth of July?" McAdam's face was cold. He did not look like a man who would entertain much nonsense.

"I am not aware of any obstruction…"

"That's not the same thing. We have passed this parade with Dublin City Council and the Gardai, and have gone to a great deal of effort and expense to lay on transport, and we expect a significant representation from our fellow citizens in the Unionist community in the North. Will they be welcome in Dublin?"

For a man who practiced and rejoiced in obfuscation and bonhomie, he was now on very uncertain ground. They couldn't allow Unionists to be attacked in Dublin. Hanna will have to be grounded. Madden poked the fire:

"Will you be signing the Affirmation?"

For the past three days, since this meeting was arranged, he had been wrestling with that very question. He was an Irishman; why wouldn't he sign a pledge of allegiance to his country? But what country? If he signed, it would be like voting Yes in a referendum to get rid of the border – and accepting the consequences. If he didn't, his farm… his family… his life!... were at risk. But how would they know whether he'd signed or not? They'd know.

He looked at Downey. Severe. She said they'd use any and all means. He had no reason to doubt; this was Endgame.

"Indeed I'll be signing. I'm proud of my country."

"Does the Taoiseach know that?" God, these were unpleasant people.

"I will be advising the Taoiseach of my intentions. I believe we are of one mind on this. It is a tremendous opportunity for the country to come together, and a great advance to be welcoming Unionist people to Dublin."

After the usual wrangling and horse-trading over portfolios, the first COBRA meeting of the Cabinet of National Unity – an emergency meeting - was called and chaired by former Minister for Defence and now Prime Minister, Pippa Baldwin.

Besides the necessary house-keeping, there was only one item on the agenda. There could be nothing else.

Before the item was tabled, Pippa Baldwin suspended Minutes and sent round a sheet of paper stating that all the undersigned hereby promised to never, *ever*, discuss the agenda of this meeting again. The doctrine of Cabinet Confidentiality wasn't sufficient;

she wanted a signed oath that would hamstring all signatories with immediate loss of office and prosecution under the Official Secrets Act. Those unwilling to sign should immediately leave the Briefing.

The paper was first signed by the Prime Minister and went round the table without debate. It was then handed to the Cabinet Secretary for filing under the 30-year rule.

The Secretary of State for the Home Department then produced a note that had been received via an MI5 dead-letter drop arranged after the Tonbridge crisis. He first explained the type-written note's origins and then read it out:

'Further to recent events in the towns of Chipping Norton, Oxfordshire, and Tonbridge, Kent, we hereby inform the British government that we will be bound to take further action unless Father Tomás Doherty, currently held in prison in Broadmoor High Security Hospital in Berkshire, is released in conditions of absolute secrecy into the care of certain neutral parties to be nominated after your acceptance of this ultimatum. Signed 'Skipping Rope'.'

"That's it. That's all it says. I think we know what it means."
"Is it genuine?"
"I've spoken to MI5. They say the source was familiar with all pre-arranged codewords and procedures. He was able to answer questions only the Anthrax bombers would know the answer to. I'm afraid we must take it as genuine."
"You know the precedent, Prime Minister; we do not negotiate with terrorists."
"I know we don't… unless they have their boot on our throat and a bloody gun pointed at our balls!" Pippa Baldwin was from up north; she had always been 'one of the boys'.
A silence descended on the room. Where would this end?

Dinner was over and a summer shower had turned the red bricks of Broadmoor into glistening black. At one end of the corridor, Jack the Axe was pacing his cell shouting for his chocolate bars. He was getting fat; they had him on a diet. At the top of the corridor, the night man was drumming his pen off the desk and flicking between the cell cameras. Not savoury, sometimes, but nothing unusual.

A red light and a buzzer; number 107, the priest! The camera panned his cell. He was crumpled over the arm of his chair. A team of three rushed in. The panic button at his feet beside his round National Health glasses. A medic hunkered down beside him; eyes bulging tongue swollen and sticking out, retching noise as he tried to vomit, snot hung from his nose "Looks like food poisoning. Call the doctor."
They moved him to the bed; it wasn't difficult; already weakened from an old shooting incident, he was not a strong man; he weighed only 115 pounds. The doctor arrived. An antihistamine to reduce swelling. "Allergic reaction. What did he have to eat?"
"Chicken. He's had chicken before."
The priest was hurried to the medical ward where he was treated for gastroenteritis. The other patients who had chicken were checked. All ok.
They kept a watch on him during the night with constant rehydration, but he was overcome by diarrhoea and vomiting and was getting weaker. A politically sensitive patient, it was decided to get him to the teaching hospital in Hammersmith for intensive care. He was taken away in an ambulance under guard. Teaching hospital records showed a patient under the name Joseph Healy from Broadmoor was admitted with symptoms of poisoning.

A train slid into the station at Coleraine. Though there were people on the platform, no one rushed to get on board. They stood back, remarking on the flags and banners that festooned the engine and first two carriages. 'IRELAND IS OURS' they proclaimed. People moved forward, hesitating at first, but then with a sense of proprietorship.

Ernie Gibson was there with his wife Dot. He was no longer a young man, and his wife was accustomed to fussing over him, what with his walking stick and his tendency to be forgetful.

But he remembered enough. He remembered when he was a young man, and a big brock of a man he was. In his B-Specials uniform, he was an imposing, intimidating figure, well suited to striking fear and reticence into the hearts of catholics that would have the nerve to deny him at a roadblock or reading out a country pub of Fenians.

That was a long time ago, fifty years, that he had enforced the Queen's Peace in the little villages and dark roads of Northern Ireland. Many a head was thumped and, God help us, two men killed.

Now in his old age, he thought about it often; the certainties, the righteousness of the times. And he wondered if it was all worthwhile. It had all been sliding downhill ever since. The Queen's Writ was on the run. Now the young king visited to see how it used to be, in the museums.

Over time, it upset him so much he asked his wife, "What is there left?" She couldn't tell him, but he had done his duty, done it well, and there's an end to it.

She read it to him in the local paper; a train leaving Coleraine to go to Dublin; on the day after the Twelfth of July. And the train said 'Ireland is Ours'. "Rubbish!" She thought she knew him well after all these years. When they drove to the supermarket, he was preoccupied. When he was sitting in his armchair, he didn't hear her talking to him; she found him in the garden, staring into space.

"We're going to Dublin, on that train."

"Are ye mad? Away out of that with ye."

"No I'm not. I've been thinking about it a lot. Something has to come out of it. They were very dark days; they were unholy. Maybe this is what was meant to be." She couldn't turn him.

She had never been to Dublin. It would have been a betrayal. They wouldn't give the papists the satisfaction.

Now they were well-seated. They were early. "Dottie, thanks for coming with me."

"You know best, dear."

"Don't worry about the neighbours, they'll have to make up their own minds… Gary says Saint Stephens Green is nice…"

"Any park is nice. Gary and John going down there for football is one thing, this is a different thing."

"Would you really care if we had a country we called ours and we were on good terms with England?"

"Well, I don't know. It might be an improvement on what we have now. You know Andy Boyd is leaving? He has a job got in Sheffield."

"Andy was always True Blue."

"Weren't we? Aren't we?"

"It is taking a chance, I'll grant you that. But the North isn't going to last. At least this is peaceful."

"We could have stayed at home."

"We could. But if you think of it this way, we're doing this for our own kind, to keep them settled, and safe."

"I hope you're right, dear."

They hadn't noticed, the train was moving slowly and quietly out of the station. In the carriage, people unpacked their sandwiches and coffee or tapped energetically on their cellphones or unrolled their copy of The Sentinel :

> '*Is this train bound for glory? Your chance to board the Takeover Train*', by Crawford Gainsworthy.
>
> The train that starts its journey from Coleraine to Dublin this morning might not be bound for glory, but it's bound to make you think.
>
> Is it a PR stunt by undercover nationalists in *The Movement*, or is it a genuine opportunity for wavering Unionists to find a lasting home on this island and be in on the ground floor on the founding of a new state, with all the opportunities that it offers?

We all know the numbers; there are nearly one million 'unionists' in the North, and a further 250,000 in the South. Taken together, they would make up about twenty percent of the total population of the island and about eighteen percent of the eligible voting population.

In a new, secular nation, if they were to vote as a block (and why would they, with allegiances irrevocably changed with the onset of Unity?), they would exert significant influence in elections if Proportional Representation (custom made for Unionists) were the method of voting.

We know the economic arguments; joint North/South enterprises would bring economies of scale and would solve the European problem, but would also bring redundancies with rationalisation.

And how would Northern Ireland compensate for the loss of the £10 billion annual subvention from the British exchequer to finance the local NHS etc?

We know the Peace Dividend. Some Loyalists would undoubtedly leave the North, many others would have to adjust their thinking (did YOU sign the Affirmation?) – something that might not be achieved in this generation.

And lastly, we know the historical baggage and folk memories - on both sides.

The South has changed (Europe, instant communication, independent thinking, the decline of prescriptive religion), while here in '*Norn Iron*', the young people look at us old ones and ask "Are you mad, with your marches and banners and your 300 year old battles, for all the good they have done you? They make for colourful parades – but let that be all."

We can consign 'No Surrender' and 'Not an inch' to the dustbin of history. Such attitudes have no relevance or constructive value any more.

So this newspaper, taking a wide view of the situation, and aware of the many unanswered questions, asks you, the reader, "Have you a better idea?" Can you take this ball and run with it, or would you prefer to wait until you are outvoted and fade away in the next generation?'

Dot handed the paper to Ernie and lapsed into silence.

The train drifted on, stopping at a series of small stations, picking up passengers. It was impossible to tell by their dress or demeanour if they were nationalist or unionist; they boarded quietly, found seats, and occupied themselves in their own affairs. The atmosphere was reserved, cautious. Plain-clothes police leaned nonchalantly against the doors.

The next sizeable station was Antrim. The platform hosted a good smattering of passengers, onlookers and media, probably 50 or 60 overall. As interviewers approached passengers for a comment, a group of Loyalist protesters in orange sashes had been pushed along the platform as more passengers arrived, and were now calling on God and the king near the Exit sign. How had they gained access to the platform without a travel ticket? passengers asked. Passengers clumped together, half expecting to be attacked or at least verbally abused. Some strained to hear the comments of interviewees while staying out of camera shot. The general attitude was tentative; maybe people would be more relaxed after they boarded the train.

In Dublin, the Lord Mayor and several Cabinet ministers convened a Welcoming delegation of the elevated and the elite at the Mansion House on Dawson Street in preparation for their march down the quays to Connolly Station in their robes and chains of office. The Sinn Fein mayor told reporters she looked forward to greeting fellow Irishmen and women from the 'six counties'. The Minister for Local Government said it was a great day for Ireland.

As the train rumbled towards Lanyon Place in Belfast, radio reports suggested that a group of loyalist youths had broken through the barrier at Newtownabbey and were intent on boarding the train. Anyone thinking of travelling had deserted the platform for the coffee shop and ticket office, having been informed that police were on their way. Aside from the protestors and media, only two other men, in suits, remained on the platform. It transpired they were members of a less-extreme Unionist faction and they were now involved in a heated debate with loyalists in full view of the media. The 'suits' were arguing for patience:

"Why don't you wait till people return from Dublin and comment on the parade rather than trying to intimidate them from going in the first place? I'm sure they're as good and loyal protestants as you. They are right to look at alternatives. Anything's better than what we have now."

"They're traitors to Northern Ireland and the flag. They're only fuckin' appeasers. They can go to fuckin' Dublin, but they won't come back here, I can tell you that."

"You're living in the dark ages, so you are."

"Fuck off. We're defending the king and our culture. What are ye doing? Now fuck off, or you'll get a kick up the hole."

At this point, a posse of police arrived in two squad cars. They moved swiftly past the ticket collector and onto the platform where the standoff had dissolved to muttering resentment. The senior uniformed officer, with definite stride, approached the protagonists: "Gentlemen, ladies, I hope we can resolve this without any further difficulty. This train will leave the station without being molested in any way, so I ask you all now to leave the platform unless you have a legitimate ticket for travel. My officers will board the train here and remain on board until it approaches the border with the Irish Republic where they will hand over to officers of the Garda Siochana. Any attempt to interfere with this train will be considered a breach of the peace and those involved will be arrested. Is that clear?"

A tall, thin man at the rear spoke up: "We are here to defend the integrity of Northern Ireland. We will have no truck with appeasers."

"You are welcome to defend Northern Ireland and you can do it in a peaceful manner outside this station. If you do not have a ticket for travel, you must now leave this platform."

A voice muttered "Traitor bastards!"

"Your tickets will now be checked."

The protestors counted the number of PSNI officers in front of them and, anticipating that there would be reserves in waiting, shuffled and mumbled towards the exit. A fat woman dressed entirely in a Union flag started upon 'God save the King'. The rest halted and were called to Attention. The PSNI officers gave them their moment of grace, leaving it impossible for the protestors to hazard which of the police might be fellow loyalists and so sympathetic to their stand.

Upon command, two officers moved ahead to make way for passengers now returning from their refuges, the train's arrival having been called on the loudspeakers.

It was now a straight run to Lanyon Place. Passing the high flats on the Shore Road, passengers were subjected to a clattering as hails of stones landed from balconies. Along the track, intermittent groups of loyal protestors took revenge on the traitors and quislings within, casting their staves and curses knowing they couldn't penetrate the ring of steel that surrounded the main station.

Despite the crowd, there was an unexpected silence at the main station. Commuters for other connections did not dally at the approach of the Glory Train, but hurried for their platforms or pulled down blinds from the security of their carriages. Stragglers moved away from the advance of the Dublin Special.

Following Newtownabbey, junior ranks and pioneers of The Movement were anxious to get on board, and the platform was soon clear. The train moved deferentially up the funnel of machine-gun-carrying police.

In London, the Prime Minister Pippa Baldwin and her ministers watched the televised minute-by-minute progress; the hot-line to the American president lay before her, primed for intervention.

There would be no stopping at Portadown; it was considered too close in time and space to Mourne Meadows and the local police commander said he could not guarantee the safety of intending travellers. These passengers would have to travel to Newry to board.

There is no physical border between Northern Ireland and the Republic. In many cases, only a change in quality of the road surface tells you that you have left one century and moved to another.

As the train slowed slightly to observe signals, a man standing in the corridor looking out the lowered window, swore: "I've just heard shots".

"No!" Another man sprang up to join him. Only the steel wheels. The two men exchanged querying glances, and the train swept on towards its destiny. Fifty yards away, across the railway track and hedges, a policeman lay wounded on an unapproved road. He struggled with his breathing, trying to understand the force that had struck him. To his left, he could see a briar several inches from his eyes. He could hear voices; just noise. The ground was dry. He couldn't smell the grass; his stuttering breath wouldn't let him inhale; he had a blockage at the bridge of his nose. The briar was hazy, then it disappeared.

Further down the unapproved road, an ambulance was nose-down in the ditch, its back doors open. Just behind, a car with a flashing blue light protruded at an angle into the narrow road. its windscreen was cracked and splintered, a round hole in the glass at the driver's side. In the driver's seat, a man stared through red and dripping eyes. In his right hand, he held his rosary and tried to pray: "Holy Mary Mother of God... Holy Mary, Mother of God..." He couldn't remember... "Holy Mary, Mother of God."

Liam Maguire, commander of the South Armagh Active Service Unit for the Defence of Ireland, 'The Border Foxes', was slumped down on the floor of the ambulance beside the dolly on which Fonsie was strapped; "Liam! Liam!" No reply. Then, from the front seat: "Fonsie, are you hurt? I'm tied in. What's wrong with Liam?"

"Liam shot".

The passenger door of the ambulance was flung open, then snapped shut again. A boot dislodged it and Fonsie's brother Johnsie staggered out and tripped into the ditch, cursing. He struggled round to the back of the ambulance and was met by Fonsie's eyes staring. "Liam's shot. Is Donal alright?"

"Dead. Fuck. Right, I'll get you out. We're only a hundred yards from the border. Hold tight."

Johnsie undid the straps locking the dolly in place and wrestled it out the back of the ambulance. Grunting and cursing, he extended the legs and got it upright. "Right, we're all off to Dublin in the green" and set off pushing the dolly down the middle of the little rough road. He knew the PSNI would send another car soon; the first cop car would have called in their position. Jovey McArdle had his petrol pumps and garage just a mile away; if they could reach it unseen...

A sign at the side of the track announced Dundalk. Dot Gibson was taken aback; she didn't even realise she had crossed the border. She wondered if the air would change. After 76 years on this earth, it was the first time she had ever been in this country. She sat quietly thinking her thoughts. The air hadn't changed, the sun was still in the sky, the grass was still green. She thought the level of conversation had risen in the carriage; she even heard a couple of laughs. People were following the news on their phones. Apparently 20,000 people were in O'Connell Street, 1000 at Connolly Station, waiting to greet the train. The ground was thick with politicians hoping to get in on the ground floor of whatever was happening. The great siege banners of The Movement were being marshalled along the quays of the Liffey river.

The Junior Minister at the Department of Foreign Affairs, who was also Dublin Lord Mayor and a Dublin city councillor, arrived at Connolly Station with the delegation from Dublin City Council to greet the visitors. Their progress down the quays had been accompanied by long banners stating 'Ireland Is Ours'; this gave room for some misgivings which were compounded when the mayor struggled to get through the crowd at the station to claim her rightful place at the head of affairs; having reached the platform, she found that the gardai had fenced off a wide semi-circle by the ticketing gates. With all the dignity her chain of office would allow, she attempted to lead his delegation into the void, but was peremptorily confronted by two Movement stewards who motioned her towards a corner outside the perimeter: "This area is reserved. You can wait there."

"But I am representing the City. We are the official delegation".

"The City is already represented. You can wait there."

The stewards took her by the elbow and guided her to the space where the TV cameras, reporters and microphones waited. She had a very fine speech in her purse, and only needed the opportunity to deliver it.

Seven minutes for the train to arrive and, on queue, a party of fifty young men and women in black pants, white blouses and their gold capes emerged from the platform and lined up to form a guard of honour. Behind them, the crowd was separated by stewards, and a multitude of flags of the raven and 4-pointed star were marched to the gates.

From afar; the train! Banners flapping, flags flying, the whistle blew its greeting, the crowd responded with a tremendous roar, the train docked.

The first passengers jumped to the ground, pumping the air in response to the welcome. Some were more cautious. Ernie climbed down the steps, backwards, partly to steady himself with the handrail and partly to keep an eye on Dot who was now seized with apprehension and hesitated in the dark doorway of the carriage.

A man and a woman were escorted from the concourse of the station to the first carriage by a liveried attendant of the railway company; there they waited while the passengers commenced to disembark. A woman of 30-ish was first to make her way down the steps of the front carriage with her folded copy of The Sentinel; the man on the platform, in a muted business suit and tie, stepped forward to greet her: "I am Robert McAdam. I am chairman of The Movement. We are the organisers of today's celebration. You are most welcome."

"I know who you are, Mr. McAdam..." A strong east-Belfast accent..."I am a Unionist councillor for Ballymacarrett. I was at the Uniting Ireland conference in Belfast when you made your speech. You're promising a lot, but I wanted to come to Dublin to see if it's worth taking over."

"You're a careful buyer."

"Indeed I am. A lot of people have asked me to suss this out, so that's what I'm doing."

By now, the remaining carriages had decanted their load and a phalanx of visitors, attracted by the strong female voice, was approaching the conversation. McAdam called: "Ladies and gentlemen, will you now join us as we follow The Movement banners to a reception at Dublin City Hall? It's your day out, it's your city, so enjoy it".

Dot had finally overcome her hesitation and was helped down the steps by Ernie. They fussed over who would carry the raincoats but, looking at the day, they agreed it was best to store them in the carrier bag for the time being. The crowd was now confidently heading for the exit, so they had to press on; if there was a time for doubt, it wasn't now.

With not a dignitary in sight, they followed the banners. People applauding along the route, fancy office blocks, the sun in the sky, the air fresh.

They crossed Liffey water at O'Connell Street. Dot was quietly grateful for a chap behind who seemed to know the place and was able to point out the sights to his companions; she didn't want to go home with one arm as long as the other; the big statue of Daniel O'Connell, Trinity College, the Old Parliament building, the Central Bank. Sooner than she expected, they came to the City Hall; she was quite pleased it wasn't as nice as Belfast's, but she was grateful for a seat inside and a nice woman came over and asked her and Ernie would they like tea or coffee or water. They were both pleased to take coffee and a biscuit. They would go for dinner later.

After a short time, the P.A. system came to life and someone introduced Robert McAdam:

"Good afternoon, everyone, and *welcome home*.

I know some of you are tired after your journey, and you'll want to rest for a while or go out and see the city on this lovely day, so I won't detain you long.

"We applaud your courage in taking this journey. This is a first step towards the resolution of division that has plagued this island for so long. We're going to change all that. Your journey and this reception is a celebration of who we are, we who Yeats called 'the indomitable Irishry'.

"It is our intention to be rid of the border forever; two borders, actually; the one on the land, and the one in your head.

"You will have many questions, many reservations, about the Health Service, the economy, education, currency, integration, nationality and so on; these will all be answered in time. As with other challenges, they will be *managed.*

"But first, and most importantly, we must *establish the nation.* Without that, the rest is superfluous.

"The nation we will make will have new structures and institutions. It will have a Proportional Representation system of voting so that all minorities will have a voice, so that the genius of the people can be applied to the progress and general good of the nation. People who now describe themselves as Loyalist or Unionist or Northern Irish are welcome to contribute as citizens to the direction of that state, but be clear: they will have no state of their own on this island. British people, of course, are welcome to continue to live in this new state, as many Irish people now live in Britain.

"The new state will have a new flag and a new national anthem to which *all* on this island can freely give allegiance. We the People will determine what they are; we will not just accept the current devices as a given. We will, of course, maintain those symbols and identifiers of Ireland which are known and admired throughout the world. We will maintain friendly relations with Britain, Europe and America.

"How do we propose to accomplish these things? It is evident that the public debate and the public support we have engendered to date have been such that our single objective of Establishing the New Nation is seen as a major stepping-off point in the debate over living arrangements on this island.

"Now, some people can not, in conscience, accommodate that objective. These people can not be allowed to hold the majority to ransom; therefore, those people will have to make alternative arrangements…

"I hope you will feel able to bring these thoughts back to your communities. At the back of this hall, you will find banks of computers. These computers hold the voting lists for both the North and South of Ireland. I invite those of you who are content to do so to find your name on these lists and sign your Affirmation of Loyalty to Ireland here today. Some will want to reflect further, and that's fine; these computerised lists will be available as we take our message to communities all over Ireland.

"Please go from here to the General Post Office in O'Connell Street where there is a great gathering of Irish people and dignitaries from England, Europe, America and the United Nations.

"Finally, let me, on behalf of all the people of Ireland, thank you and applaud you again for taking this initiative, and for your concern about the future of your country. Until we meet again…"

The people were white, the sky was blue, she could understand the natives, but Dot couldn't bring herself to sign, even as they found their names and address under Belfast South. Ernie was torn; he didn't want to offend his wife of fifty years; he was aware that some friends in Belfast were already planning to move to England and Scotland; he was aware that the paramilitaries, and some old colleagues, in East Belfast and in the countryside were planning an armed response. He was also aware that the IRA would not do anything to interfere with the Loyalist reaction, leaving Loyalists having to decide who to fight against, thus reducing their cause and support even further. He didn't want it all to end in war at his age; he would rather see his days out in peace and quiet. They decided to think about it.

Ernie still wanted to see that place where his queen had made peace with her dead enemies, but he knew it would be asking too much of Dot. So they walked down Dame Street to see the statues in St Stephen's Green.

Following voting, the Glory Train passengers wearing the enamel badge they had been given as a memento of the day, moved at a leisurely pace towards O'Connell Street where the would hear short speeches of welcome from, among others, Lord Penrith from the British Upper House and Rapporteur of the International Committee on Co-operation of the EU, John Patrick Dannagher, Under-Secretary of State at The Treasury of the USA, Maria-Joseph Martinez, Office of the Secretary General of the United Nations. Each speaker looked forward to the day Ireland, as a single, united and peaceful community, would take its honoured place among the nations of the world.

In response to questions, Mr. Dannagher said it was premature to discuss a 'Marshall Plan' for a united Ireland, but there certainly was a great preponderance of opinion in the USA in favour of a successful resolution of the 'border question' and the large Irish-American constituency would carry considerable weight in any administration.

All were thanked by the joint Chairs of the meeting and were urged to go forth and 'spend a few Euros' in the pubs, shops and cafes of Dublin, and be sure to be at Connolly Station by 6pm for the return trip to the North.

O'Toole had parked his car just north of Belturbet on the M3 so that DD and her friend and part-time bodyguard, Frankie McLurg, could continue on to Derry while O'Toole took left at Enniskillen for Bundoran. Sharing a car to and from Dublin was a sensible arrangement and there were animated discussions of the day's proceedings. It had been an emphatic success. O'Toole found he could participate wholeheartedly in the banter and chat.

They pulled in beside O'Toole's car which appeared to have survived unmolested, and he gathered his bits and pieces. Hearty goodbyes, and Frankie moved off. For a moment, O'Toole thought that DD might have glanced at him with something more than camaraderie, but he put it out of his mind and thought instead of what he'd have for dinner. He couldn't be bothered to cook, so he'd treat himself to fish & chips as a reward for a good day's work. He ate a sandwich, then set off. The remains of the day would be pleasant.

Half a mile up the road, and he couldn't see DD's car any more; they had sped on. He changed the station on the radio and was cruising when he saw the tail of a red car, just like DD's, stopped up a lane, surrounded by police. In the process of reversing, flashing appeared in his mirror; an unmarked police car. He stopped, and the unmarked car reversed. O'Toole reversed, and turned up the lane; he knew what was going on. He pulled up behind DD's car - they were still inside - and got out, ready for a row. And there, approaching him in his familiar greatcoat, Superintendent Hanna.

"Mr. O'Toole, so nice to see you after all this time.I thought you'd deserted the Old Sod, and done a runner… No? Anyway, nice to see you."

"What are you doing, Hanna?"

"It's lucky you're here, really, to witness the apprehension of the miscreants who attacked a garda officer. You remember your friend Michael Devlin, of course? Struck down at a parade run by these cowboys."

Just at this point, Frankie McLurg, the bodyguard, was ordered out of the car by a garda officer. As he came out, he was met by a crunching blow to the head from a police baton and slumped to the ground with one foot still trapped inside the footwell.

"Naughty boy", observed Hanna, "resisting arrest."

"Hanna, arrest that officer. That was blatant assault…" O'Toole's remonstration was met with a severe blow to the backs of his legs which sent him to the ground in an ungainly heap as his legs folded.

"Tut tut. You should know better than to interfere with a police officer in the execution of his duty," and he turned to the officer commanding the passenger door of the red car. "Get her out."

The officer opened the door and attempted to pull Doreen Downey out of the car. With a cry of pain, he pulled the point of a tara brooch out of the back of his hand. "Bastards! Bastards!" The passenger door flew back and forth as DD attempted to knock the gard out of the way. McLurg's assailant came round to grapple with her, and dragged her out, cursing and screaming.

"Excuse me, old chap." Hanna went to where the gard had pinned DD's arms behind her back. "Mrs. Downey, I must confess I've never liked you," and he drove his fist into her stomach. Downey groaned and fell silent. He returned to O'Toole who tried, but was unable to rise. "You people are causing problems, Mr. O'Toole. You're rocking the boat. We don't like that much down here, so we are glad we have found the two people responsible for that attack on Garda Devlin. And they just happen to be big noises in The Movement. Isn't that unfortunate? It will be the first item on the news tomorrow morning. So I'll tell you what, O'Toole; you toddle on to Burndoran, I'll be taking these two with me. I wouldn't complain if I was you; nobody would believe you of all people and you'd only make yourself a, eh, a target, Yes?" Hanna smiled his smug smile and, spinning round, kicked O'Toole full in the stomach. He signalled the gards to pull him out of the way of the cars; they dragged him to the side and dumped him in the ditch. They put Downey and McLurg into separate cars and drove off.

O'Toole knew he wasn't seriously injured, but temporarily helpless. Who to call? Maire? He didn't know how long he had been down, but the air was light and birds were singing. As he attempted to come to terms with his pain, doubled-up in his ditch, he heard tyres on gravel and registered a rusty grey van on the skyline. "Good God, who is it now?"

Surprises, like magpies, are sometimes better when they come in pairs. The van drew up beside him and he could see two feet landing from the passenger side of the van. He followed their progress around the vehicle. "O'Toole! In trouble again?" Staring down from a great height, Chief Inspector McConaghie.

You didn't have to be that bright to figure it out. He always knew he was being watched. Being in the company of some of the people most dangerous to the status quo in Ireland must make him a marked man. "How did you know?"

McConaghie glanced to the sky and made a circling movement with his finger. Drone. No hiding place. Technology marches on.

O'Toole, still in his ditch: "Where's the other cars?"

"We have them at Belturbet." O'Toole didn't ask if they were all right. McConaghie would have told him.

"Where's Hanna?"

"All locked up in a blue van, heading for Dublin."

O'Toole stretched in the ditch and assessed his chances of rising. Probably ok now. McConaghie would see a pathetic man dragging himself out of a drain. It didn't matter now. This is how it ends. "What now?"

"Go home. You'll be met at the border by your old Brit friend D.I. Scouse. He'll say hello and set you on your way. He'll wait for Mrs Downey and Francis McLurg and have a word with them. They've gone to a doctor in Belturbet for a check-up. He'll decide if they need the hospital. Scouse will see them back to Derry. It might be more than they deserve, but Hanna went overboard, so we've given them the benefit of the doubt."

O'Toole noted that McConaghie hadn't yet enquired about *his* health, so no need to be too grateful. He followed McConaghie to the rusty van, noting the TV screens and electronics in the back as McConaghie got in. "We'll see you in Bundoran tomorrow about a statement."

Although it was painful, O'Toole tried to scan the sky; only the darting birds. But they were watching up there, somewhere. He knew that. The game was changing. McConaghie hadn't asked about the letter; maybe *it* was sacred.

The next morning, he awoke early and turned on the radio, still lying in bed. The Minstrel Boy. He'd have to phone Maire, just in case there was anything on the news. Success in Dublin would give The Movement respectability. The Gardai would be coming for their statement; he'd have to take them off the premises; can't upset the customers or give them too much to talk about. DD would make contact to make sure he still had the letter. Her own discomfort from the incident wouldn't be of any consequence. In fact, if McLurg was ok, she probably wouldn't even mention it to her family. This was no time for adverse publicity.

He got to thinking about his chat with Scouse; a coalition government in England and the threat of The Sanctuary Knocker.

We're all on the edge. He would consider his own part in the piece later, when peace descended. Checkmate.

The 7 o'clock news came on from Dublin. The Glory Train had returned to Belfast and Coleraine unmolested. There was no account of Hanna's arrest. The Taoiseach was quoted as pronouncing The Movement gathering as 'a welcome to fellow citizens from the North.' His forté was in blowing with the wind. Politics, isn't it?

Two PSNI officers killed near the border, apparently in a shoot-out with 'terrorists' who burst a burns patient out of hospital in Newry. The shop would be buzzing with news. Enough to be getting on with on a Monday morning.

He struggled his way out of bed.

Given his appearance, an obviously diseased man, and deathly sick, they took no chances, and fumigated and deep-cleaned his cell. Some other lunatic would get a shiny new home to take the place of the deceased. Thallium poisoning, in the chicken. It was no surprise; they were out to get him. Priest bastard! Killing those kids in Oxford. He was no loss.

They wouldn't miss Joseph Healy either. Had worked on the sites for years. Drank all his money on a Friday night. Never saved enough to go back home. Asbestos on the lungs. Pity really, but that's the way it goes. Had an elderly brother in Kerry; they were trying to make contact. The brother would be too old to travel. The church in Quex Road, Kilburn, had a benevolent fund for distressed Irish citizens. They'd bury him.

An ambulance was dispatched on that early October evening and negotiated the chaos of rush-hour traffic on the Hammersmith roundabout. When he should have taken the Shepherd's Bush turn-off for Kilburn, he continued around and eventually exited at the A4 Great West Road, travelling west. An onlooker would have assumed he'd taken the wrong turn in the fog. He'd have to turn around at Hogarth Lane. But he stayed on the A4 and was moving west at speed, way off course.

Half an hour later, he was seen on the Southern Perimeter Road hard by Heathrow airport. He swung right into the cargo area and, presenting credentials, was waved on to the tarmac where a private plane waited.

Two men descended from the back of the ambulance and helped a third across the tarmac. The third man negotiated with some difficulty the steps of the plane. Ten minutes later, they had secured a take-off slot, and the plane climbed away from England, destination Paris.

The Vincentians, a Roman Catholic Order, was founded in Paris in 1625 for the purpose of preaching to the poor, providing sanctuary and alms to the beset, and educating young men in seminaries. Having survived the French Revolution and other difficulties, it spread its good work throughout the world. In modern times, it maintains its connection to Paris with its motherhouse on Rue de Sèvres in the 6th Arrondissement.

On this chilly night, the superior general of the Order waited alone by the heavy door below the statue of the founder, St Vincent de Paul. Eventually, a people-carrier pulled into the front courtyard and the man with round National Health glasses stepped down with a small suitcase and was absorbed into the shadows, there to see out his days in silence.

~ THE END ~

Printed in Great Britain
by Amazon

80308333R00078